Thomas felt his breath catch in his throat.

Abigail had turned her face up to his. A smile danced across her expression, and she had a healthy glow—a maternal glow.

He swallowed the lump and stepped back, bumping into the buggy.

"Something wrong? You looked like you'd had a fright."

"No. Nothing to be afraid of. I was just...um... looking at the window displays—nice fall stuff."

Abigail laughed. "Didn't guess you to be a window-display kind of guy."

Her laughter felt good, so much better than the look of despair on her face that Thomas had seen when he first arrived that morning. The day wasn't going at all like he'd planned...

Not that he was getting involved. Because spending too much time with Abigail would not be prudent. Hopefully within a few months the estate would be settled, she could hire permanent workers and Thomas would be on his merry way.

Except suddenly that didn't sound as appealing as it usually did...

Vannetta Chapman has published over one hundred articles in Christian family magazines and received over two dozen awards from Romance Writers of America chapter groups. She discovered her love for the Amish while researching her grandfather's birthplace of Albion, Pennsylvania. Her first novel, *A Simple Amish Christmas*, quickly became a bestseller. Chapman lives in Texas Hill Country with her husband.

Books by Vannetta Chapman

Love Inspired

Indiana Amish Brides

Visit the Author Profile page at Harlequin.com.

An Amish Baby for Christmas

Vannetta Chapman

LOVE INSPIRED
INSPIRATIONAL ROMANCE

LOVE INSPIRED®
INSPIRATIONAL ROMANCE

Recycling programs
for this product may
not exist in your area.

ISBN-13: 978-1-335-40951-5

An Amish Baby for Christmas

Love Inspired
22 Adelaide St. West, 40th Floor
Toronto, Ontario M5H 4E3, Canada
www.Harlequin.com

Printed in U.S.A.

Give, and it shall be given unto you;
good measure, pressed down,
and shaken together, and running over.
—*Luke* 6:38

Learn from yesterday, live for today,
hope for tomorrow.
—Albert Einstein

This book is dedicated to Beth Scott,
a faithful reader and dear friend.

Chapter One

Thomas Albrecht was walking out of the grocery store, juggling three full-to-the-brim grocery bags, when he practically ran into his bishop. Ezekiel Hochstetler had recently turned eighty—Thomas had been there to help celebrate the day, along with their entire community.

Ezekiel's only concession to his age was a cane, which he now used to help with a knee that had been giving him trouble. Thomas understood that the man in front of him was having a hard time learning to step back. He'd only recently delegated a few of his church duties to his deacons because his wife had insisted. Ezekiel continued to preach and counsel and generally oversee his flock.

"Morning, Thomas. I was hoping to see you today."

"Were you, now?" Thomas nodded toward his buggy. "Let me set down these supplies. I note a twinkle in your eye, which I suspect means you have a new job for me."

"Finished at the Beachy place?"

"Just yesterday. Fall crops are harvested, and the winter wheat is in the ground."

"Are you looking for another job?"

Thomas set the groceries in the bin on the back of his buggy, closed the top, making sure the latch fastened, then turned to study his bishop. Both his hair and his beard were pure white. He was dressed in the typical Amish way, the same way that Thomas was dressed—white cotton shirt, black work pants and the requisite suspenders. Ezekiel wore his black Sunday hat, while Thomas wore his straw one. Both men had their shirt sleeves rolled up to the elbow. The Plain community in

Shipshewana might have embraced solar power, but they still dressed in the traditional manner.

Ezekiel was more than his bishop. He had been a friend to Thomas for many years. It was Ezekiel who had first suggested that Thomas begin a property management business—an unusual profession for an Amish man, but Shipshewana had been at the point of growth where it was needed. The idea had been a wise one. Thomas had never lacked for work.

Thomas crossed his arms and leaned against the buggy box. "Tell me what you have in mind."

"Do you know Abigail Yutzy?"

"*Nein,* I don't." Thomas tipped his hat against the bright sunshine. They were deep into September, and in northern Indiana that was a thing of beauty. The trees boasted vibrant colored leaves, every porch sported a collection of pumpkins and the weather remained perfect.

"I'm not surprised. She lives on the east

side of Shipshe, so she's technically in the other district."

"Widow?"

"*Ya*, she is."

Most of the women that Thomas had worked for in the past had been widows. Their living situations were usually stuck in some phase of transitioning. Most were post-funeral but hadn't yet sold the family place to move in with one of their children. Thomas liked to think that he was able to help make that transition less traumatic, less difficult.

"Her situation is somewhat...unusual." Ezekiel didn't add anything else, and Thomas knew that questioning him would be futile. Often these situations were sensitive. Thomas would learn more about the particulars of Widow Yutzy as it became necessary.

Ezekiel pulled a slip of paper from his pocket and handed it to Thomas.

"This is Luke Fisher's number. He's the bishop of the east side group. He actually has a cell phone." Thomas winked. "They're a bit more liberal than we are."

"And you think I should call?"

"I told him you would."

Instead of being offended that Ezekiel had spoken for him, Thomas laughed. Ezekiel knew him well. He wouldn't turn down helping one of the older members of their community.

He stuffed the slip of paper in his pocket. "I'll do it."

He thought that would be the end of the conversation, but Ezekiel tapped his cane against the ground. "Today, if you could. The situation is a bit…dire."

"Before lunch," Thomas promised.

He hurried home to his apartment above Lehman's Mercantile. He was perhaps the only Amish man in the district who lived in an apartment, but the arrangement worked well for him. The Lehmans' house sat on the back side of the property. Beside it was a medium-sized barn that housed their buggy horse as well as Thomas's mare, plus some goats, a dairy cow and whatever animals the children persuaded their parents to let them keep.

The mercantile was a busy place, which didn't bother Thomas at all since he was rarely home during the day. After he spoke with Bishop Ezekiel, Thomas hurried home to his apartment, made his way up the back stairs and put away his groceries. Then, he went down to the office in the mercantile and asked to use the phone.

"Of course, Thomas. New job?" Though Mary Lehman was only forty-five, her brown hair was liberally streaked with gray. She had taken to wearing reading glasses that hung from a braided ribbon. Now she positioned them on the end of her nose and studied him.

Thomas thought if there was a sweeter woman in the town of Shipshewana, he'd certainly never met her.

"Maybe."

"Well, call then. We don't want you starving."

That was a standing joke between them. Mary insisted on feeding him at every available opportunity. Just the week before, he'd accused her of attempting to fatten him up for the winter.

Now he called the number on the slip of paper Ezekiel had given him. It was unusual for a bishop to have a cell phone, though plenty of Amish had one for their business. He could understand how it would help a bishop who was basically on call twenty-four hours a day. No doubt the man kept it in his barn rather than the house—a concession to the old ways and the sanctity of family time.

He was surprised when Luke answered on the second ring. Unfortunately, the connection was a bad one, and the man's voice kept cutting in and out. He was travelling in his buggy, evidenced by the background sounds of automobiles, wind and the clip-clop of a horse.

"I'm Thomas Albrecht. Bishop Ezekiel Hochstetler asked me to call you about helping a widow."

"Oh *ya*. Very *gut*. Asher Yutzy...crops

are still…she won't…if you could go by…
goat…help her…"

"This connection isn't very good. What
was that you said about a goat?"

The bishop must have reached the top of
a hill, because suddenly his voice was as
clear as if he were standing in the mercantile office. As he gave Thomas the address
for the Yutzy place, Mary slipped a pad
of paper and a pen in front of him. Then,
the connection dropped completely, and
Thomas was left staring at the receiver.

"What did he say? Was that Bishop
Fisher? I heard that he's using a cell phone
now. Apparently, that way he's available
whenever his congregation needs him."

"He may be available, but that doesn't
mean they'll be able to understand him."
Thomas handed her the phone as he
frowned at the piece of paper. "He asked
me to help a Widow Yutzy. She lives on
the east side of town."

"Different district, then. I haven't heard
of her, but that's no surprise the way this
area is growing. Did you know there are

twenty thousand Amish in the LaGrange-Elkhart Counties now?"

"I did not."

"I'm lucky to keep up with the people in our own church. Where exactly does this Widow Yutzy live?"

Thomas showed her the address.

"Huh. That's the east side, all right—nearly halfway to LaGrange."

"I suppose that's where I'm headed, then."

"Chicken and dumplings for dinner," Mary called after him. "And Chloe is making peach cobbler."

Thomas winced at the mention of Mary's daughter, Chloe. She'd had a rather pronounced crush on him for the last two months. Chloe was fifteen, and Thomas was twenty-eight. Soon he'd be too old to be the recipient of schoolgirl crushes. The day couldn't arrive fast enough in his opinion. Chloe's current infatuation would pass. These situations always did, but until Chloe turned her attentions elsewhere, he was better off avoiding the Lehmans' dinner table.

Too bad. He would have loved to have a bite of that peach cobbler, and Mary's chicken and dumplings was one of life's blessings. He momentarily considered braving Chloe's pointed looks and long sighs, but shook off the idea. He could make himself a sandwich with the groceries he'd just purchased. Chloe was bound to move on to a boy closer to her own age soon. He'd wait her out.

The Yutzy place might have been on the east side of Shipshe, but it was still a relatively short trip. Shipshewana was, after all, small. The number of people living in town remained under eight hundred—an even mix of Amish and *Englisch*. County numbers were just under forty thousand, and a vast majority of those folks were Amish. In the last ten years, the area had become something of a tourist attraction for *Englischers* curious about Plain living. The auction house and flea market consistently attracted crowds of an additional thirty-five thousand. Still, on days the market was closed, Shipshe reacquired its small-town feel.

After Thomas had traveled east for six miles, he stopped to ask for directions.

"Big place that Asher Yutzy had. Real shame about his passing." The man tending the vegetable stand was in his sixties. He nodded back toward the main road. "Keep following this road until you see the county number on the left. Yutzy's place is the second on the right. You can't miss it. Asher had dreams of starting a horse farm. He put that newfangled PVC fencing around the entire two hundred and twenty acres."

Thomas had been inspecting the man's produce, thinking that Mary would enjoy some of the fresh green beans. He nodded toward a quart-sized tray. "I'll take those and some of the berries too. Did you say two hundred and twenty acres?"

"I did. Asher had a different idea of plain and simple than most folks."

Even with the man's warning, Thomas

was surprised when he pulled onto the lane that led to the Yutzy property. Most Amish farms were eighty to one hundred acres— never more than a family could manage. The idea was to provide for your household and make a modest living from the land. Amish farmers would hire help during harvest, but it was rare to hire full-time, permanent workers. Growing a vast agricultural empire wasn't the point of farming.

Enough land to raise a family.

That was their motto.

It was obvious the late Mr. Yutzy had different thoughts on the matter. Though the entrance was plain enough, the white fencing stretched as far as he could see in both directions. Thomas had priced the fencing for a farm on the north side of Shipshe. It had been exorbitantly expensive. In the end, they'd gone with metal T-posts and goat fencing, because…well, the man had goats.

Why would Yutzy have spent the money on PVC? And why did he have such a large spread? Perhaps the man had a houseful of sons and planned to divvy it up between them. But if he had sons, then Widow Yutzy wouldn't need Thomas. Ezekiel had said it was an unusual situation.

Thomas called out to his horse, Duchess, directing the chestnut mare down the lane. She was a fine horse—with a beautiful gray coat and black socks. He realized it was a sin to feel pride, but he didn't figure it was a sin to appreciate God's creatures. At least that's the way he justified his satisfaction with the horse.

A lovely September day.

A mare that tossed her head, but followed his lead.

And a new job.

September was progressing on a good note. He pulled up in the circular drive—it was dirt, of course. No Amish home had paved driveways that he knew of. But this one had a center garden area that had once probably looked quite impressive. Like everything else, it had been sorely neglected.

The house was small in comparison to

the size of the farm. He was surprised to see the fields had yet to be harvested. In addition, a glimpse of the back garden revealed a mess of weeds and vegetables that needed to be collected. Then there was the goat standing on the front porch, munching on what might have been dead flowers in a pot.

Perhaps Widow Yutzy wasn't physically able to take care of the place. But if that was the situation, then their bishop would have sent help.

Something else was going on here, though he couldn't imagine what.

He climbed the porch steps, shooed the goat away, knocked on the door and then stepped back. Thomas wasn't extraordinarily tall at five foot eleven inches, but his size sometimes intimidated people who didn't know him. He was built solid as an ox. His *mamm* had loved that phrase, though now that he thought about it, she'd also called him "clumsy as an ox."

The woman who answered his knock was younger, so a *doschder* perhaps. She opened the front door and peered through the screen at him.

"My name is Thomas—Thomas Albrecht. Your bishop asked me to come by. He said you might be needing some help around the place."

She shook her head, still studying him, still silent.

"I couldn't help but notice as I drove in that your alfalfa hasn't been harvested. You'll need to see that's taken care of soon."

"*Danki*, but *nein*. I don't need your help." Her voice was soft but brooked no argument.

Which left him in something of a pickle. He'd told his bishop and her bishop that he'd do his best to help.

Perhaps he could reason with her.

"After the harvest, I suspect you'll want to put in a cover crop or maybe winter wheat. Then there's your vegetable garden in the back. I can take care of all that as well and..."

"I don't need your help." Since she was standing in shadow, he couldn't make out her expression, but her tone suggested she was determined to turn him away.

"Your fields tell a different story."

She pushed out through the screen door, and you could have knocked Thomas over with a flyswatter. The woman had dark brown hair, a good bit of it escaping from her *kapp*. She was probably half a foot shorter than he was, and her eyes were the color of hazelnuts. Though she was slight in most ways, she was also very pregnant. Certainly, she was in her last trimester. Perhaps she was past due. He didn't see how her stomach could get any larger. Plus, she was barefoot. Who walked around barefoot in mid-September? It was warm, but it wasn't that warm.

Taking two steps back, he averted his eyes to a spot over her left shoulder. "Perhaps I could speak with Widow Yutzy."

"*I'm* Widow Yutzy."

"But—"

She stared up at him, arms crossed protectively on top of her stomach. "I'm Widow Yutzy, and as I've told the *gut* bishop before, I'm not ready to decide on what type of help I'd like, when I'd like it or who I'd like it to be."

"Then how will you—"

"I'll manage. I always manage." Her voice drifted away as her gaze focused on something past him.

Thomas turned to see what she was looking at, but all he saw was what he'd noted before—fields in need of harvest, a horse that was in the pasture and a near-perfect September day begging him to get to work.

Widow Yutzy stepped back into the house, allowing the screen to close between them. "*Danki* for the offer. Now, if you'll excuse me, I was in the middle of something."

Without another word of explanation, she firmly shut the door.

Abigail stood near enough to the window that she could watch Thomas Albrecht shake his head in disbelief, walk slowly down her porch steps and climb back into his buggy.

Good.

Good riddance.

Unfortunately, as soon as he stepped off the porch, that stupid goat returned. She needed to find a way to keep that beast off her porch and out of her flowers.

Tears stung her eyes, but she refused to let them fall.

Probably just baby hormones.

One hand on her stomach, she whispered, "No worries, little one. No worries."

Thomas Albrecht turned his buggy around and headed back down the lane.

Wunderbaar.

He'd been easy to scare off.

Ha. One look at her stomach, and he'd nearly fainted.

She didn't need a strange man's help. Plus, this fellow was a big guy. She had to look up at him to meet his gaze.

What was Bishop Luke thinking, sending someone like that out to her place? And who was Thomas Albrecht? She'd never seen him before; that was for certain. She would have remembered. He had to be close to six feet and over two hundred pounds, though from what she could tell that weight was all muscle.

She walked back into the kitchen and stared at the pile of bills on the table. She needed to take care of them. The crops in the field could wait, but she had to figure out Asher's system for paying bills, and she needed to do that today.

A cup of tea. That's what she needed. A cup of tea and a few minutes off her feet. Who would guess that a person's feet could swell so much? She pulled the canister of tea bags out of the cabinet, dropped one into her favorite mug and filled the teakettle with water...and that was when she glanced out the window.

She couldn't believe it.

He was back! Thomas Albrecht was back, and that stupid goat was still there—once again munching on her dead flowers!

She grabbed the broom as she exited the kitchen and headed toward the front porch. All she could think of, all she could see, was that goat. He made red dots dance in front of her eyes. Regardless how much she stomped or hollered, he came back. She'd even tried beating a spoon against a pot, but the goat had only stared at her and pulled up a chrysanthemum.

No matter what she tried, the goat always won, but not today. She'd had it. She raised the broom and proceeded to take wild swings at the creature when suddenly the broom was pulled from her hands. Thomas set the broom against the porch banister and made a noise in the goat's direction.

The goat never looked back. The beast jumped off the end of the porch and sauntered away.

If she wasn't so irritated with Thomas Albrecht, she'd ask him to teach her to make that noise. Instead, she turned around, plucked the broom from where he'd placed it and wondered if she could sweep him away.

"Maybe I wasn't clear before."

"Oh, you were clear."

"Then why are you back?"

"Because your fields still need harvesting." Thomas yanked off his hat, revealing brown hair that had a surprising curl to it. "Just hear me out."

"Why should I?"

"Because I have something I need to say."

Which stopped Abigail in her tracks. She understood the need to be heard. How many times had she wished Asher would just listen to her? Thomas couldn't have known that. He couldn't have guessed that he'd poked one of the sore spots in her heart.

"Fine. Have your say, but I need to get off my feet." She collapsed into a rocking chair and stared down at her feet in despair. They didn't even look like feet. They looked like puffballs.

Thomas let out a whistle. "So that's why you're not wearing shoes."

"Couldn't get them on. Not even close."

Thomas started to say something, then stopped.

"Go ahead and say it. You can't make matters worse."

"I was just going to ask you to stay put for a minute. I'll be right back."

In three long strides he was down the porch steps and headed across the yard. He made that noise to the goat again, but this time the beast followed him.

"Where is he going?" Abigail spoke to her baby. That's what she told herself, anyway. It was better than admitting that she talked to herself quite often.

She closed her eyes, grateful for the cool breeze. Who would think that September could be so warm? Wasn't fall here? The leaves had turned orange and red and brown. They looked ready to abandon their perch, to fall to the ground in a cascade of color. She should open the windows in the house. Right after she made her tea. With open windows and a cup of tea she could face the pile of bills.

She must have dozed off, because the next thing she knew, Thomas was back on the porch, carrying a large bucket filled with water.

"Try putting your feet in there. The water from the pump was plenty cold."

She wanted to argue with him, but what was the point? Instead, she slipped her feet into the water and a sigh escaped her lips.

"I should have thought of that."

"It's a fair walk to the barn."

"Especially if you're barefoot."

"Especially then." Thomas pointed to the other rocking chair. "May I?"

"Sure. Why not."

"Explain to me why you don't want your fields harvested. If it's a matter of money, I'm sure your community's benevolence fund will cover the cost of my work."

"It's not about the money." Which wasn't exactly true, but he didn't need to know the particulars of her situation.

"What, then? Because if we don't harvest it soon, before the rains start, you're going to have an even bigger problem on your hands."

Instead of meeting his eyes, Abigail picked at a spot on her apron. When was the last time she'd done laundry? What was wrong with her? Tears again stung her eyes, but she bit her lower lip, corralled her emotions and finally looked at the stranger sitting next to her.

"Why do you care?"

"Your bishop called my bishop. I live in Shipshe, more on the west side—well, northwest. Anyway, apparently Luke called Ezekiel and said you needed a hand." He hesitated, then added, "He said it was a bit of a special situation."

"What is that supposed to mean?"

"I was hoping you could tell me."

Abigail wanted to answer. The man sitting next to her was pushy, but plainly he meant well. The problem was where to start. How did she begin to explain that she was good and stuck? She seemed literally incapable of making a decision. Had nine months with Asher completely dissolved her backbone? Or was it the baby? She honestly didn't know.

Apparently growing tired of waiting, Thomas cleared his throat and barreled forward. "Needless to say, when our bishops mentioned Widow Yutzy I was expecting someone older."

"Sorry to disappoint you."

"I certainly wasn't expecting someone..."

"Pregnant?"

"Ya."

"And yet, here I am."

"Look." Thomas leaned forward, elbows on his knees, fingers laced together, and waited for her to turn her attention to him.

She wasn't used to that—a man waiting for her attention, a man interested in her opinion. She had forgotten what that felt like.

"I don't know your...situation, but this sort of thing is what I do."

"This sort of thing?"

"I'm a property manager...for Plain folks."

"I've never heard of that."

Thomas smiled and leaned back, set the chair to rocking. "We sort of made up the position."

"We?"

"Ezekiel and I."

"Your bishop?"

"*Ya*, but he's also my friend. He's been more of a father to me than...well, than my own father."

Abigail wiggled her toes in the water, then pulled her right foot out. Surprisingly, the swelling had gone down. She wanted to tell this man that she was just fine on her own, but plainly that wasn't true. She wanted to stand up and assure him that she didn't need any help, but she'd be standing, barefoot, wearing a dirty apron, in the bucket of water he'd fetched—all pointing to the fact that she did need help.

"All right," she conceded. "But just the harvest. Those other things you mentioned...cover crops and vegetables. I'm not ready to decide on those yet."

It was obvious that Thomas wanted to argue with her. He opened his mouth, shut it, then stared at his work boots for a moment. Possibly he was smarter than he looked.

"Just the harvest, then, and after that we'll talk."

"Deal."

Thomas studied the sky. "Rain's predicted for early next week. I'd like to get this done before that happens. Hopefully, I can assemble a work crew by tomorrow."

"Is a work crew really necessary?"

"Looked like a large field. How many acres are planted?"

Abigail shrugged. Whenever she'd asked details about the farming side of things, Asher had changed the subject.

"I'll need a couple of extra hands, at least. Don't worry about the money. I'm sure Luke will—"

"I have plenty of money." Didn't she? Asher had never acted as if money was a problem. He'd dressed well, their house was adequate and he'd talked on and on about his plans for the farm. "Just let me know what I owe you when you're done."

Thomas's right eyebrow shot up in confusion. And he swallowed the question he wanted to ask. He almost looked comical sitting there, full of energy and ideas, yet unsure how to convince her to let him attack all the chores. Apparently, he decided that fight was best left for another day. And why should he even care? He was doing a favor for his bishop or hers. That didn't make him responsible for her farm.

He nodded and stood, proving he was wise enough to know not to push her. "Do you need help getting inside?"

"I'm not sick, only pregnant."

"Does that mean you don't need help?"

If she wasn't mistaken, there was a twinkle in his eyes. Smart with a sense of humor. Why wasn't he married? No beard, so she knew he wasn't. Perhaps he was courting. That would explain it. A long courtship.

"I believe I'll sit here and enjoy this cool bucket of water a few more minutes."

Thomas fetched the broom she'd left leaning against the wall of the house and handed it to her. "In case that goat bothers you again."

She watched him climb up into the buggy,

watched the pretty chestnut mare toss her head and trot down the lane. She watched Thomas ride off into a picture-perfect September afternoon.

She wished he'd never come.

She wished with all her heart that he wasn't coming back.

Abigail wanted to do this alone. She needed to do this alone. Hadn't her *mamm* said as much in her last letter? It was in there, on the table, buried by the bills.

I didn't have help at your age, and it made me stronger. This will make you stronger, Abigail Marie.

Abigail didn't feel stronger. It had been four weeks since her husband's death. Four weeks since she'd found herself alone in a town where she had no family or friends. And now Thomas Albrecht had appeared on a bright fall day to offer his help.

Perhaps her *mamm* would have had her out pulling in the harvest herself, but Abigail knew that wasn't going to happen.

Thomas could harvest her field. She'd pay him, and then he'd be on his way. She'd be alone again. Alone and getting stronger, if her *mamm* was correct.

Time would tell.

Chapter Two

The next day Abigail woke feeling marginally better.

Perhaps Thomas had shaken her out of her stupor.

Regardless of the reason for her sudden clarity, Abigail understood that her first step in righting her world would be to visit the bank. It wasn't going to be an easy thing to do. Of course, she knew how to hitch a horse to a buggy. The problem was that she didn't think she could manage it. Her stomach was too big. And although her feet were less swollen than the day before, she still had trouble walking in her shoes.

As she ate a breakfast of tea with dry crackers, she contemplated her options. Should she split the shoes down the side with a knife? Then she'd have to buy new ones. On the other hand, she couldn't wait any longer to go to town. Several of the bills were already past due. She certainly couldn't go barefoot.

She spent an hour going back and forth on a plan of action.

In the end, she pulled out an old pair of Asher's work boots. They were too big, but she stuffed socks in the toes and wore them anyway. So what if people laughed at her. Most people would never get past staring at her whale-sized stomach. There was little chance anyone would notice her feet. She had managed to hand-wash her aprons the previous evening. It was easier than trying to work the gas-powered washing machine.

She had two dresses that she could still fit into, so she picked the one that she hadn't worn the day before. Stuffing the stack of unpaid bills along with Asher's checkbook into her purse, she trudged out the front door. Thomas had arrived at daybreak. She'd watched from the kitchen window as he and three other men headed out into the fields.

That had been several hours earlier, and she hadn't seen him since.

Time to figure out what to do about harnessing the horse.

She nearly made it to the barn before Thomas spied her.

He said something to the other men, then jogged over to where she was standing.

Abigail cinched her purse strap up over her shoulder. "How's the work going?"

"*Gut*. It's a big field, but we'll be done tomorrow."

Her heart sank. She'd hoped she would be rid of him by the end of the day. Still, she should be grateful, so she plastered on a smile and said, "I'll leave you to it, then."

He didn't return to the field.

He followed her into the barn.

"I see you have your purse."

"I do."

"And shoes."

So much for hoping no one would notice she was wearing Asher's shoes.

"Are you headed somewhere?"

"*Ya.* I have some business to take care of in town."

She stopped by the buggy and pulled in a deep breath. She could do this. She *would* do this.

"What's the mare's name?"

"My mare?"

"Well, I know my mare's name. It's Duchess."

"Fancy name."

"I didn't give it to her. That was her name when I bought her." But he smiled good-naturedly before asking again, "And your mare?"

"Belle."

"Belle's a fine name. I'll hitch her up for you." Without waiting for Abigail's response, he left to fetch the horse.

Belle was an American Saddlebred, and Abigail had fallen in love the first minute she'd laid eyes on her. The mare was a reddish brown with white markings along her nose and back. She was a *wunderbaar* horse. When Abigail had first moved to Indiana, when the loneliness felt like a weight around her neck, she'd often spent hours brushing Belle.

Abigail liked to think that she and the horse had an understanding. Belle would tolerate the extra attention in exchange for a special treat—a carrot or piece of apple or even a peppermint. She'd purchased a bag of those when buying groceries. Asher hadn't been happy about that. "Real waste of money," he'd said. Belle disagreed.

Thomas fetched the horse, harnessed her and hitched her to the buggy. Turning to Abigail, he held out a hand to help her up into the seat.

How long had it been since she'd touched another person? Asher had been dead less than a month, and yet Abigail felt as if she'd been living inside a bubble of grief and disbelief all of her life. She pushed those thoughts away, put her hand in Thomas's, and the bubble of grief burst.

Or at least it seemed to for a moment.

He smiled. "Have a *gut* time in town."

"Danki."

"Gem gschehne."

The dread she'd been struggling with fell away as she directed Belle down the lane. The day was autumn bright—blue skies as far as she could see and lawns dotted with red, yellow and orange leaves.

She was almost able to forget the nightmare of the last few weeks.

Then she drove into town and pulled into the parking lot of the bank. She swallowed the bile in her throat—the dread and embarrassment.

Abigail had no trouble standing up for herself. She'd been forced to since she was very young. Growing up, her *mamm* had insisted that there would be no coddling in their home. "Learn to handle your own messes." That had been a favorite saying of hers. If someone was being mean to her at school, she could speak with them or the teacher. There were times when Abigail had felt too young and completely inadequate for the small problems of life, but each time she'd stood up for herself.

Today was no different.

The problem was that she was unfamiliar with most of the things she had needed to do since Asher's death. She'd never opened a banking account. Her parents had insisted that she didn't need one, and Asher had told her not to worry, that he would take care of everything.

"So much for that plan," she muttered, climbing awkwardly out of the buggy, clasping her purse to her side and walking bravely to the front door of the bank.

Ten minutes later she found herself in the office of the vice president. Jayden Webb looked to be in his forties. He had dark skin, his black hair was cut close to the scalp and tinged with streaks of gray and he wore a suit and tie.

What had she expected?

That he'd be wearing farming clothes like Thomas?

She shook the thought from her head and

took a deep breath. Time to explain her situation to this stranger.

"My name is Abigail... Abigail Yutzy. My husband, Asher, died on the twenty-ninth of last month."

"I'm sorry for your loss."

"*Danki*. I mean, thank you."

His tone was truly sympathetic, which caused tears to sting Abigail's eyes. She looked down at her purse, gathering her thoughts once again.

"The thing is, Asher was only forty-eight. We had no idea that he had a medical condition. The heart attack was... It was a surprise. We weren't..." She studied the wall behind Jayden Webb, searching for the right word and finally settled for "prepared."

That was the understatement of a lifetime.

"Asher was a valued customer of this bank. I've met with him several times myself. He was an aggressive businessman, but as you said...there was no indication that he knew of the heart condition." Mr.

Webb picked up a pair of glasses, opened a folder and stared down at the papers there.

Abigail had an insane urge to snatch them away and run out of the room. Instead, she cleared her throat and pulled out the stack of bills along with Asher's checkbook.

"The thing is that I have all these bills, and I have Asher's checkbook, but my name isn't on the checks."

Now Mr. Webb shuffled through the papers, searching for something. Not finding it, he flipped the stack over and checked again, then pivoted to his computer. After he'd tapped a flurry of keystrokes, he shook his head once, and turned his attention back to her.

"He didn't put you on the account."

"Excuse me?"

"It's not that uncommon with our Amish customers. Often the man takes care of the business side of things, and in many cases the wife doesn't even want her name on the account. You wouldn't believe how many times I've counseled families about the need to have both names on the account or at least to have a beneficiary form filled out. Asher didn't do either of those things."

"What does that mean?"

"It means that I can't give you access to the funds in his account."

"*Our* account."

"Technically—*his*, for now."

Panic clawed at Abigail's throat as she pictured giving birth to her baby out in a field because she'd been kicked off the farm, or worse yet...going home to her parents. It was an unkind thought, but there it was. She would have chosen the field over her parents' farm. She didn't want to birth her child or to raise her child in a home that didn't know how to show affection.

"What do you mean *for now*?"

Instead of answering her question, Mr. Webb pressed the tips of his fingers together and studied her. Finally, he asked, "Did Asher have any other children?"

"*Nein*. He'd not been married before."

"Which isn't the same thing, but for

now we'll let that be. Are his parents still alive?"

Abigail shook her head. Asher had told her very little about his parents, but she knew they'd perished in a bus accident when they were visiting cousins out of state.

"Then based on my knowledge of the laws of Indiana, you will inherit all of his estate."

"Which includes what?"

"Everything—the land, monies in his accounts, etcetera."

"I can use the funds in the account to pay these bills?"

"No. You can't."

Abigail wasn't very good at hiding her emotions, and she had no doubt that her dismay was written across her face. She sensed that Mr. Webb was a compassionate person and understanding of her situation. She also recognized that a bank was a business, not a charity. He would go by the book.

He opened his desk drawer and pulled

out a business card, then passed it to her. "Mrs. Yutzy, I suggest you speak with a probate lawyer."

"I don't want a lawyer." She stared down at the small business card, her frustration growing as tears blurred her vision. "I just want to pay my bills."

"But you need a lawyer because you won't have access to Asher's money until his estate is probated."

"How long will that take?"

"Generally? Two years."

Now anger replaced her dismay. "What am I supposed to do until then? How am I supposed to pay these bills? How do I provide for my child, for Asher's child?"

Mr. Webb's tone softened. "I can only imagine how hard this is for you, Mrs. Yutzy. Contact the name on that card. An attorney can request an emergency injunction and petition the court to give you access to Asher's funds until the matter is settled." He waited until she nodded, then he stood, effectively dismissing her.

She'd barely made it to the door when he called her back.

"May I make a suggestion? Speak to your bishop. He'll help you through this. You're not the first young woman, young wife, to be in such a situation. It's best if you don't try to navigate what lies ahead alone."

Abigail fled the bank, ignoring the gazes that turned her way as she rushed out the door and into the parking lot. She stood there, trembling and lost and angry all at the same time. She should have felt better back out in the sunshine.

She didn't.

So instead, she walked over to her mare and stood there a moment, brushing Belle's neck and breathing in the smell of her. She was in this alone—with only the baby and the horse to help her through the days ahead. It was as if her mother's dire warnings had come true.

Learn to handle your own messes.

It looked like she would have to, though she had absolutely no idea where to start.

Her only idea had been the bank, and that had gotten her nothing other than a business card for an attorney that she couldn't possibly afford to hire.

Thomas kept an eye on the lane. He wouldn't put it past Abigail to attempt to unharness the horse herself, then sneak into the house. And he suspected she could handle the mare, but he couldn't shake the image of her in her freshly laundered apron and *kapp*, wearing a pretty blue dress and her husband's shoes. A woman who was about to birth a child shouldn't be struggling with a mare's harness.

His own father had done little to instill in him the proper way for a man to handle responsibilities, or perhaps his lack of example made him work harder to understand responsibility. Maybe it was because he'd had to be the man of the house sooner than most that he understood the importance of helping one another, of standing together, of being supportive. Regardless of the reason, he couldn't leave until he saw the horse cared for and pastured, and Abigail safely in the house.

The other men broke off work at three in the afternoon since they needed to go home and tend to their own chores before dark.

"See you tomorrow."

"Don't finish the field without us."

"*Ya*, no hogging the work."

There was laughter and waves as they walked toward their buggies.

Thomas had only met the men that morning. The bishop had put out a call the night before and they'd shown up carrying a lunch pail and wearing a smile. That was the way of Plain communities. Thomas wasn't a bit surprised, and he'd immediately liked Jonas, Benjamin and Abe.

So why hadn't they already harvested the field?

Why were Thomas's services even required?

The deacon in charge of benevolence should have already taken care of everything that Abigail needed. He hadn't, though, which left two possibilities. The first was that the deacon was incompetent, but after two conversations with Bishop Luke, the man didn't strike him as someone who suffered fools. The other possibility was that Abigail had refused help.

Why would she do such a thing?

He couldn't come up with a single answer to that question that made sense.

Instead of brooding over it, he focused on making himself useful. He cleaned out Belle's stall. It wasn't in terrible shape, which meant someone was stopping by to take care of mucking it out. Still, he cleaned it again, spread fresh hay, filled the water trough and made sure oats were in the bucket for the mare.

Everything progressed smoothly despite the goat. The goat was a real pest.

He stuck his head in the oats bucket, spilling a good bit on the floor of the stall.

He managed to climb into the water trough.

"I was warned about you." Thomas studied the goat. Something was agitating the beast—even for a goat, his behavior was beyond obnoxious. He'd come across troublesome animals before, but this one was winning the prize for Most Irritating. Why was he so intent on being around people?

Thomas leaned against the wall, crossed his arms and watched the animal. The goat raised his head high and made a sound like a child, then lowered his head and butted a bucket until he'd succeeded in knocking it over.

"I saw hay in your feeder outside, so I know someone's feeding you."

The goat again bleated loudly.

"Okay. I take it you're not impressed with the hay. Let's have a look around."

As he walked through the barn, the goat followed him. The structure was larger than most and well organized. Even from the outside, it looked to be in better condition than the house. He'd yet to see the inside of the house, but the inside of the barn shouted that this was Asher's priority. It didn't take Thomas long to take an inventory of Asher's supplies. He found what he was looking for within ten minutes. On one of the higher shelves—where goats couldn't reach it—was a large bag of black oil sunflower seeds. Thomas had barely managed to pull it off the shelf when the goat began nudging him.

"This is what you want?"

He reached into the bag and pulled out a handful. The goat made fast work of it and looked at him as if to say, "That's it? I've been waiting for weeks."

"I guess you were a little spoiled."

He spied an old Tupperware container, filled it with the seeds and walked out of the barn. Sitting down on an overturned crate, he put one more handful on the ground.

"That's it, though. Obviously, you were overindulged by Asher Yutzy. Wouldn't be right for me to go and make the matter worse." As he snapped the lid back on the container, he heard the sound of a horse coming down the lane, and then Abigail came into view. He held up a hand so she'd see him, and he motioned for her to stop outside of the barn.

"I'll take care of Belle." One look at her tear-stained face told him that the day had not gone well. "What happened?"

"What happened?"

She tumbled awkwardly out of the buggy—moving faster than he would have thought possible, considering her size—then she proceeded to lead Belle into the barn.

"I'll tell you what happened. I'm destitute, that's what. Broke. My pantry is basically empty, I have no money left in the cash jar, and now I have to hire a lawyer."

Belle tossed her head, agitated by Abigail's tone.

"I can't even write a check. How's that for wonderful news?"

Belle jerked her head away from Abigail. Thomas put a hand on the horse's neck and spoke gently, calming her. If only he knew how to calm the woman standing in front of him. He didn't, though. All he knew was that when his *schweschdern* were agitated, they drank tea.

"Want some tea?"

"What?" She looked at him as if he'd slipped in Belle's stall and covered himself in muck.

He glanced down. Nope. No dirtier than usual.

"Tea won't fix what's wrong here." Her bottom lip began to tremble. "I don't know of anything that will fix it."

And then the tears were streaming down Abigail's face, and Thomas had the irrational urge to pull her into his arms. Instead, he tightened his hold on Belle's harness. "I'll take care of the mare. Maybe you could go inside and...make some tea?"

"You want me to make tea?"

"*Ya.* That would hit the spot. I'd love some."

She rubbed her eyes with the palms of her hands, reminding him of a child. But she nodded. And she turned and walked from the barn.

Thomas turned back toward the mare.

"Whew. I don't know what that was about, but seems as if we barely avoided a full meltdown." He'd never have said that to his *schweschdern*. They'd have taken him to task for it and reminded him of all the times that he'd lost control of his emotions—which hadn't been often but also hadn't been never.

Belle nodded in agreement, so he knew he was right. He took extra care putting up the harness, checking the buggy to make sure everything was fine and settling the horse. Best to give Abigail a few minutes to pull herself together. When he estimated that twenty minutes had passed, he shooed the goat out of the barn, shut the door and walked across to the house.

Abigail wasn't sitting in the rocker on the porch, so he knocked on the front door.

When she didn't answer, he opened the door and stuck his head inside. "Hello? Abigail? Can I come in?"

The only response was more muffled sobs.

He hadn't given her long enough.

He couldn't very well walk back over to the barn now. It was obvious he'd finished with the work there. He honestly didn't have a lot of experience with crying women, but there also wasn't anyone else around to take care of the situation. Maybe he could pour her a cup of tea.

He wiped his feet on the mat and called out that he was coming inside. Peeking into the kitchen, he saw Abigail sitting at the table, her arms crossed on the smooth oak, head on top of her arms, and sobbing sounds coming from her general vicinity.

Fortunately, the teakettle whistled at that very moment, so he didn't have to think of anything to say. Abigail didn't act as if she'd heard it, so he strode across the kitchen, found two cups and a tin of tea bags—noticing as he did so that there was very little food in the cupboard. He plopped the bags into the cups, added hot water and then took them to the table. He'd like to have put out some crackers or cookies, but he didn't see any. What was this woman eating?

He sat down across from her and waited.

Finally, she raised her head, but she still didn't speak.

"Try the tea. It's *gut*."

She shook her head, but then apparently changed her mind. After she'd taken several sips, she blotted her eyes with her apron and thanked him for the tea.

"Well, technically it's your tea."

"*Ya*. Probably the last of it too."

"There's three more bags in the tin." Why had he made himself a cup? He was an idiot. He made a mental note to bring tea from the mercantile when he came back the next day...and groceries. Would that be crossing a line? But plainly she did need groceries. Perhaps he should simply stop by Bishop Luke's on his way home and let him know the situation.

"I don't know what I'm going to do."

"Maybe you should tell me what's wrong. Or better yet, I could fetch the bishop for you."

"What's wrong? You want to know what's wrong?" She found her *kapp* strings and wrapped them around her palm—forward and back, forward and back. "What's wrong is that my husband didn't bother to put my name on the bank account, so I have no money. According to the bank's vice president there are funds in the account, but I won't be able to access it for maybe two years."

"Asher didn't have a will."

"He did not."

"And now you have to probate the estate."

She looked at him quizzically. "How do you even know about such things?"

Thomas shrugged. He didn't want to go into the fact that his father had left his mother in the same situation after his years of drinking and disappearing for months at a time. His father had a sickness, and he understood that, but at the same time that sickness had hurt a lot of people. Settling his estate, which contained precious little, had put an added burden on his mother both financially and emotionally. He understood all too well what the woman sitting across from him was going through and what she had ahead of her—at least financially.

Abigail covered her face with her hands. Her shoulders shook, and it sounded like she was weeping again. Thomas felt real pity for this woman, but he didn't think that her present attitude was very helpful.

"You need to stop crying."

Her head jerked up, and she stared at him. "Excuse me?" There was a bite to her tone, but he preferred it to the expression of hopelessness she'd had on her face since coming home.

"I said you need to stop crying."

"I can't believe you're speaking to me in that manner. What are you? An ogre?"

Thomas rubbed his chin, then attempted a smile. "I've never been called that before."

"Surprising."

"It's just that crying isn't helpful."

"You're not helpful."

"Actually, I just harvested your field, stabled your horse and, by the way, I also took care of your goat problem. Turns out he was used to getting a handful of sunflower seeds every day."

"Sunflower seeds?"

"*Ya.* I left a container full on the shelf where you put the horse brush."

Abigail stared at the ceiling, her brow furrowed. "I couldn't buy peppermint for Belle, but he could buy sunflower seeds for the goat?"

"I don't understand."

"Never mind." She turned her gaze back to him. "Why are we even talking about my goat?"

Thomas shrugged. "At least you've stopped crying."

Abigail sat up straighter and fiddled with her cup, turning it left, then right, before finally downing what was left of the now-cold brew. "Let me guess. You're not comfortable with emotional women."

"Well, I have three *schweschdern* who

occasionally turned on the waterworks when we were growing up."

"Waterworks? That's a stupid term, not to mention a bit callous."

"I could usually avoid their emotional meltdowns."

"This is *not* an emotional meltdown."

"It sure sounded like one."

"You are making me so mad." She actually slapped her palm against the table.

It would seem that she did have some spunk. That was nice to see.

"And you can stop smiling."

Instead of answering her, he stood and rummaged through the kitchen drawers until he found a small pad of paper and a pen.

"Here."

"What am I supposed to do with that?"

"Start writing a list."

"A list?"

"Of everything that's wrong. Then we'll address them one by one."

"I don't need your help," she whispered.

"I'm here, though, so..." He motioned to the paper.

Abigail shook her head in exasperation, but she picked up the pen and began to write.

Chapter Three

Abigail couldn't believe that Thomas Albrecht had told her to stop crying. She'd thought Asher was insensitive, but good grief—he'd at least had the decency to leave the room when she was having an "emotional moment." How she'd come to hate that term.

But why was she crying?

She was usually a practical person.

No doubt the baby hormones were to blame. She couldn't do anything about those either. So perhaps doing something—doing anything—would help. She'd make Thomas's stupid list. Fine. Then he'd agree that her situation was hopeless, wish her a good evening and go home to his nice little house and a girlfriend who was probably waiting on his visit.

When she'd finished writing, pushing so hard with the pen that no doubt she'd left indentations all the way to the bottom sheet of the pad, she tossed it to his side of the table.

He raised an eyebrow, but pulled her list closer and began to read aloud.

"Unable to access banking account. Can't pay bills. Need a lawyer. Need groceries. Not ready for baby. Probate could take two years. Two years!!"

Thomas looked at her. "You repeated that and then followed it with two exclamation marks."

"Because it's a problem."

"All right. Let's start with that one, then. Why is it such a big problem?"

"Because I have to eat."

"You know the church will make sure you have what you need."

"I don't want—"

"Help from others?"

He shrugged his big, muscular shoulders, something she found particularly irritating—both the shrug and the shoulders.

"You might not have a choice, and sometimes *Gotte* uses our troubles to make us humble."

"Do not tell me this situation is for my own good."

"Gotcha."

"Gotcha?"

"It's an expression. It means I understand what you're saying."

"Oh, I don't think you do. How am I supposed to run this farm? I can't even sell it. I can't do anything until the estate has been through probate. Mr. Webb was very clear about that."

Thomas stared down at the table for a moment. He pulled a sheet of paper off the pad and scribbled some numbers. They were sitting close enough that she could see he was adding the numbers, then subtracting others and occasionally even crossing some out. Finally, he seemed to come to a decision. He folded the sheet of paper he'd written on and stuffed it in his pocket. Then he raised his eyes to hers.

"I could work without being paid."

"Why would you do that?"

"Because I know you're good for the money. Obviously, this is a profitable place." He waved a hand toward the window. "*Gut* fields and all."

"You would work for free?"

"Not free, just..."

"A very late payment on your labors."

"I've saved up some money."

"What were you saving for?"

"A farm."

"Where do you live now?"

"Above the mercantile." He shifted uncomfortably in his seat. "Say, this discussion isn't about me. Can we get back to your problems?"

"I need to know why you'd be willing to put off your own plans—your own farm—to help me. That's sort of an important thing for me to understand."

"As I said, I live above the mercantile—Lehman's Mercantile. Do you know it?"

Abigail shook her head. "I don't think so."

"It's a nice place, and I like living above the store, plus I've grown very close to the Lehman family..."

"But?"

"But every Amish man who doesn't already own a farm is saving for one—in my experience." He fidgeted with his empty teacup, which looked ridiculously small in his large hand. "I enjoy my apartment, though I don't plan to live there forever. Still, purchasing a farm isn't something I planned to do in the next six months or even the next year. I could live on my savings while I work for you."

"You have that much saved?"

"I could also take on other small jobs. Your place is big, but I think I'd have time for that."

Abigail stared at him openmouthed.

Then she snapped her mouth shut and crossed her arms.

He waited as Abigail mulled over his answer. None of this made any sense to her. Why would he make such a sacrifice for her? He didn't even know her. She shook her head once and felt the baby push against her right side. She placed a hand there, imagined her palm up against her child's tiny hand.

"Everything okay?" Thomas's expression of embarrassment had turned to outright worry.

"Fine. Just the babe pushing on my side."

"Does it...hurt?"

"It's uncomfortable at times, but if I put my hand there then she—or he—seems to relax and the pressure eases a bit."

He shot a glance to the window, no doubt wanting to run.

The man sitting in front of her seemed to be comfortable harvesting a field or harnessing a mare or even calming a goat, but any talk of babies caused a look of panic to cross his face.

How would he manage working on her farm? And how could he do so without pay? What was the deal with Thomas Albrecht? Why was he willing to put off his own dreams and plans for what could possibly turn into a two-year wait?

For her? He didn't even know her.

He'd given up on waiting for her to accept his offer, apparently deciding he needed to be more persuasive. "Two years is probably the longest something like this takes. No doubt, Mr. Webb gave you the worst-case scenario. The estate could be probated in as little as eighteen months or even a year."

She studied him, really studied him for the first time. Maybe he wasn't quite right in the brain. He seemed capable enough, but he was entirely too optimistic. What made him think that anything would turn out better than it had in the past? What made him so confident? That confidence, almost cockiness, was another quality about him that irritated her, along with his strong shoulders.

"Back to your list. The first two things—" He tapped the pen against the paper. "Your name isn't on the account?"

"*Nein*, it's not."

Let's see how he was going to smugly solve this, which was an uncharitable thought. She realized that, but at the moment she was so tired and annoyed too. He acted as if she should be able to think her way through this. Thinking didn't change facts!

"Obviously, you can't pay your bills."

"Obviously."

"What did Mr. Webb suggest?"

"That I hire a lawyer—a probate lawyer. How am I supposed to do that without money?"

"The deacon who handles your benevolence fund will give you the money—for the bills and the lawyer."

"But I don't want charity."

"What choice do you have?"

This time she let her head fall back and stared at the ceiling. Maybe she'd find a better answer there. Nope. Nothing. A cobweb that she should wipe down with the broom. That was it. No answers.

"You can pay it back, you know."

His tone was softer, gentler. She sat up

straight and crossed her arms on top of her stomach. "What do you mean?"

"Well, any help you receive from the benevolence fund wouldn't be a loan. I don't think Plain churches make loans. It's a gift free and clear when they help church members. But you can make a contribution when you have the money to do so. You can give a gift back to the fund—an amount similar to the gift you've received. In that way, it kind of is a loan."

"I'd feel better about that. I could even pay a little more—like with an *Englisch* loan."

"Pay interest." He grinned at her.

"Exactly." When she thought of it that way, it didn't bother her as much.

"Accepting help from the community would take care of the bank account, the bills, the lawyer and the groceries. What have you been eating?"

She waved away his question.

"All that leaves is preparing for the baby." He cleared his throat and tugged at the collar of his shirt.

"Are you blushing?"

"Nein."

"You look like you're blushing."

"I don't know a lot about *bopplin*, not having any myself."

"I guessed as much."

"Did you, now?"

"You don't have a..." She rubbed her chin.

"Ah. No beard. Right. No *fraa*, no *bopplin* either, but I do have nieces and nephews. What...uh...what did you mean when you added this to the list?"

"It means I'm not ready. I don't know where I'm going to have the baby—whether I'll have a midwife come here or go to a birthing center or maybe even go to a hospital. Asher said he'd take care of that too. Trust me, Asher liked to take care of things."

Thomas looked at her curiously, but he didn't contradict her. Probably that was what prompted her to explain.

"We didn't really know each other—not well. We wed less than a year ago, and he was…well, he was busy a lot on the farm. I don't feel like, like I really knew him. Do you know what I mean? Like sometimes you can live with a person, but not know who they actually are down deep."

Thomas nodded slowly.

"Anyway. I don't have baby clothes or a crib. I thought we'd decide all those things together, and now the baby is due in eight weeks…"

"Eight weeks?"

"I'm pretty big, Thomas. I'm not sure that I'd want to carry this child around for more than nine months."

"*Ya.* Um…that makes sense." Clearing his throat, he stood, collected their mugs, walked to the sink and rinsed both of them. He seemed more comfortable on the other side of the room. Was he afraid she was contagious? That was silly. That was her being prickly, as her mother had so often accused.

"Bishop Luke's wife will help you with all those things. You know she will."

"But what I don't know is…"

"If you want her to help?"

"You make it sound so simple, but you're not the one having to depend on the kindness of others."

Instead of answering, Thomas dried his hands on a dish towel, walked back to where she was sitting and squatted down in front of her. "We've all had to do that at one time or another, Abigail. I have, my family has and now you are. That doesn't make you less in any way. It makes you human."

He waited for her to nod, then stood and retrieved his hat from where he'd set it on the table. "We're square?"

"Square?"

"I'm asking if it's all settled. I'll work your farm, and you'll pay me when the estate is probated. We'll settle on a fair price another time...when you're less..."

"Emotional?"

"Tired."

What could she do? It was a kind offer, and she had no alternatives. She'd hoped to be rid of him, but at the same time, she couldn't take care of the place alone. She didn't see as she had any alternative to what he was suggesting, so she nodded.

"And you'll speak to Bishop Luke and his wife tomorrow? Share your list with her? Let them help you?"

"Yes. All right. I'll do that." With some effort she managed to clamber to her feet, and the babe again pushed against her right side. Abigail rubbed the spot in soft circles. Was it a hand or foot she was feeling? Was it a boy or a girl?

"Do you have something to eat for dinner?"

"*Ya*. There are still a few casseroles in the freezer. I'll heat something up."

"Promise?"

"Now you're treating me like a child."

"And don't start crying again."

"You're awfully bossy."

He nodded, as if he'd heard that particular accusation before. "See you tomorrow?"

"If you're sure you want to work on a Saturday."

"I'm sure."

"Then, yes. I'll see you tomorrow."

After he'd left, she waddled across the room and watched out the window. What a strange man. Why wasn't he married? Why didn't he have his own place? Who was willing to work for two years before they were paid?

A little voice in her head suggested that perhaps *Gotte* had sent Thomas to look over her, to help her.

Her mother's voice drowned out that thought. *Learn to handle your own messes.* Her problems were still her problems. Thomas probably couldn't be depended on. She best not grow used to having him around the place, though she had to admit he'd been quite helpful so far.

Then she remembered his impatience and the way he'd told her to stop crying.

His tableside manner could use a little work.

But she did feel better, she admitted to herself. Instead of attempting to defrost and heat up one of the casseroles, she opened the refrigerator. It was nearly empty, but there were eggs and a little cheese and butter. She still had a few slices of bread. She'd make herself a nice omelet, then she'd go take a bath.

Heading to bed early wasn't out of the question.

The day had been too full and more difficult than she'd feared. Thomas's confidence in her church was all good and fine, but she didn't know if they actually had the money to help her. She didn't know the status of the benevolence fund.

She'd find out tomorrow, though, because although he'd irritated her greatly, Thomas was correct about two things. She needed help, and she didn't really have any other options.

Thomas drove home, wondering what kind of mess he'd managed to jump into. Not just any disaster either, but one that could last two years. He'd worked on many different farms, but he'd never worked at any single place for longer than six months.

He wasn't worried about the money, not really. He'd been truthful when he said he'd managed to save quite a bit. Jotting down the numbers on the sheet of paper and subtracting what he'd need had simply bought him time to think. But he hadn't needed that time. He'd known it was the right thing to do.

So what was bothering him?

He thought of Abigail, sitting there weeping at the table. He remembered the way she'd glared at him, and the one time she'd managed a smile.

He didn't know the particulars of her situation, not really. But he did know that he didn't want to see Abigail weeping. It hurt his heart. It reminded him of his own *mamm*, when she'd been left alone with a house full of children and no resources.

He'd been so frustrated then, because he was young and unable to help. Because he didn't know what to do to make things better.

But he wasn't a *youngie* any longer.

He could help Abigail. He *would* help

her. Then when she was on her feet again, when her child was born and her legal matters were resolved, he'd move on to the next farm and the next job. He didn't have to get emotionally involved.

He could stay aloof.

He *would* stay aloof.

Because the last thing Abigail Yutzy needed was to be saddled with a guy like him. His father's blood ran through his veins, and he knew firsthand what kind of damage his father had done. *Nein*, he wouldn't wish that on Abigail or any other woman.

It was the reason he'd remained single.

The reason that he hadn't purchased his own place.

Though he'd told Abigail he was saving for a farm, in truth he didn't have the courage to purchase one. He didn't need the temptation. Even the possibility that he could have a family and settle down might entice him to consider dating someone seriously. For some people that was all right, for most people in fact.

Not for him, though.

The risk was too high.

He'd run her farm, stay away from the house and Abigail and the child. He wouldn't play with her heart or his own. He'd stick to his plan.

Live a quiet, solitary life.

Help others.

Repeat.

He could work for her for two years without becoming emotionally involved, though perhaps he should avoid having tea in the kitchen with her. He just needed to stay in the barn and fields. Duchess tossed her head as if she read his mind.

The one thing Thomas was certain about was that both he and Abigail would be happier if he kept his distance. That decided, he went home to his apartment, but he didn't go inside. The thought of making himself a sandwich did nothing for his appetite. He kept envisioning Abigail's empty cabinets.

Did she really have casseroles in the freezer or was she simply telling him that so he'd leave? The one thing he knew already about Abigail Yutzy was that she was an independent kind of person. Well, he could relate to that.

So instead of stopping at his apartment, he clicked his tongue to Duchess, who happily passed the mercantile and continued down the road. By the time they arrived at Lily's home, the sun was beginning to set.

His *schweschder* had six children, ranging in age from six years to eight weeks. She was round and short and happy. She reminded him of the quintessential Amish woman—one you might find on the front of a tourist brochure, her back discreetly turned away from the camera.

Lily had married Josiah when she was eighteen. Those rare moments when Thomas felt unsure about his life, he visited Lily. She had a way of helping him see things from a different perspective.

The first thing she did when Thomas walked through the door was try to drop Fremont into his arms.

Thomas held up his hands in an I-surrender gesture.

"Oh, come on."

"You know I don't hold them until they're a little more...stable." The last thing he needed to do was break a baby.

Josiah laughed and accepted his eight-week-old son from his wife. "*Ya, ya.* You're afraid of babies. We remember."

Josiah Beachy was a *gut* brother-in-law. He was slightly shorter than Thomas and seemed to be gaining weight with each *boppli* that was added to the family. He was also a hard worker, a *gut* provider, and he had an easygoing personality. More importantly, Thomas knew that he adored Lily.

"Why are you afraid, *Onkel* Thomas?" Abner was sitting on the couch holding a library book. "For sure, Fremont won't break, but he might poop while you're holding him."

The oldest of his nephews rolled his eyes and made an exaggerated grimace that caused his younger *bruders* to burst into giggles.

Lily tickled his stomach, then turned back to Thomas. "Josiah was about to sit down with the boys for their reading time. You can stay with them or help me in the kitchen."

"I'm up for kitchen duty." When he walked into the other room, he almost took those words back. "Did someone have a food fight in here?"

"I have six boys, in case you forgot. I'm lucky there isn't food on the ceiling." She handed him a dish towel as he peered up at the ceiling. "You start with the countertops and table. I'll get to work on the dishes."

At first, he was too busy to have a meaningful conversation. Scrubbing spaghetti sauce from every conceivably flat surface took his full attention. But by the time he'd joined her at the sink to dry and put up dishes, they'd made it through the weather, the pups in the barn and Bryant's new teeth.

"I know you didn't come for a Beachy

family update." She nudged her shoulder against his. "So why are you here?"

"I like Beachy updates."

"Uh-huh, but you were just here for dinner on Sunday, so there isn't that much to update you on."

Thomas shrugged his shoulders, feeling fourteen and tongue-tied.

"Must be serious. Let's change places."

"Huh?"

"Scrub on this pan. It will help release your pent-up emotions."

"Who said I had pent-up emotions?"

Lily smiled and handed him the scrubber. It was surprisingly soothing to scrub the bits of spaghetti sauce from the pan. So much so, that he scrubbed the top of the stove as well. Lily didn't comment on that, only raised her eyebrows and said, *"Danki."*

"Gem Gschehne."

She finished drying and putting dishes in the cupboard, then stepped into the sitting room. "Everything okay in here?"

"Gut. Everyone has read their book, and

I was just resuming our story." Josiah's voice sounded sleepy. "We're on chapter three of Shiloh."

"*Wunderbaar.* Try and stay awake. Thomas and I are going to have coffee on the porch if that's okay."

"If that's what you want to do, but you're going to have to catch up on the adventures of Shiloh on your own."

Thomas didn't have to peek into the other room to know what he'd see. Lily's children loved their bedtime stories. They'd all be crammed onto the couch next to their father, the oldest probably holding the baby. How many times had he been the one reading the story? Especially after a new baby was born, he liked to stop by and give Josiah and Lily a break. Tonight, they seemed to be coping with their growing family rather well, other than the disaster in the kitchen.

He pulled two mugs from the cabinet and filled them with decaffeinated coffee as Lily fetched a tin of peanut butter bars.

Thomas ate two on the way to the back porch.

"Didn't you eat dinner?"

"Nein."

"Why didn't you tell me? I could have made you a plate of spaghetti."

"There were leftovers?"

"Hmm. Now that you mention it, *nein*, they're weren't."

"You're a *gut* cook."

"Those boys would eat anything I set before them. They have a bigger appetite than you did as a teenager."

When Thomas didn't respond to the teasing, she stared at him solemnly over the rim of her coffee cup. Josiah had placed small solar lights around the edge of the porch. They provided enough soft lighting to keep someone from tripping—and to allow Thomas and Lily to see one another.

"This must be serious."

He'd sat in the rocker, and she'd taken the porch swing. The night had settled around them, and Lily draped the blanket she had brought over her shoulders. To Thomas the cool air felt good. It helped to ease his restlessness.

"You have a *gut* family, Lily. I'm happy for you."

"Uh-oh. That sounds like you're having a midlife crisis."

"I'm only twenty-eight."

"And yet you always were ahead of your time." She sipped the coffee. "Spill it. What's going on? What's happened since Sunday?"

He told her everything—about showing up at Abigail's expecting an elderly widow, about Abigail's situation and his promise to help until she could settle her legal problems. He'd expected Lily to chide him for that—helping others was to be expected, but working for free for two years was above and beyond. Lily didn't comment on that, though. She made sympathetic noises and motioned for him to keep talking.

He described the empty cabinets and the nearly depleted tea tin and the fact that she couldn't even wear her own shoes. Finally, he ran out of things to say. Exhausted, he broke off another piece of peanut butter bar and stuffed it in his mouth—only this time it tasted like sawdust.

"Wow, Thomas."

"That's it? That's all you have to say? Wow?"

Lily's laughter loosened the tension in his neck. Lily had always been able to make him laugh. Even when they were children, huddled in the barn and hiding from their drunken father, she had been able to pull a smile from him.

"I'm a bit short on wisdom today. Sorry…"

"I hear a *but* in that sentence."

"*But* it's plain that you care about her."

"Care about her?" He popped out of his chair. "I hardly know her. If I care about her, it's in the same way I care about all of my clients."

"Are you trying to convince me or yourself?"

"I don't need to convince anyone." He had moved to the porch railing and stood there with his back to her, staring out at the darkness.

Lily walked to his side and slipped her arm through his. Thomas again felt as if they were children.

"She reminds me of *Mamm*." The confession felt like a betrayal. Why was it that even now, five years after his mother had died, he still felt a pang in his heart at the thought of her?

"Because of her situation?"

"I guess."

"Neither *Mamm* nor your Abigail…"

He winced at the *your*.

"Neither are the first Amish women to be unprepared for their husband's untimely death. For that matter, *Englisch* women experience the same."

"But most *Englisch* women have their names on the bank accounts."

"True. I've heard we Amish are a little slow to change." She squeezed his arm, then returned to the porch swing to fetch the blanket she'd left there. Picking it up, she folded it neatly, then tucked it under her arm. "Abigail sounds a bit spunkier than *Mamm*."

Thomas turned to study her and nodded once. "I suppose she is."

"She's going to be okay, Thomas. It sounds to me like you set her on the right path. Her bishop will see that she's taken care of, and you'll be there to run the farm as long as she needs you. That was a kind thing for you to do—quite the commitment to make."

Thomas shrugged. It hadn't felt kind at the time. It had simply felt like the right thing to do.

"Now come in and help me put the children to bed."

"Isn't it enough that I cleaned up your kitchen?"

"It is not. I don't know why you won't live with us. We could use your help every evening."

"Which is why I don't live with you."

Her laughter slipped through the night. Thomas grabbed the two youngest boys and tucked them under his arms, as if he was carrying two rolled-up rugs. He bent and kissed baby Fremont, who he was determined not to hold until the child was unbreakable. David and Elliott squirmed under his arms as he carried them back to the room they shared, laughing and squealing and causing his heart to swell with happiness.

Fifteen minutes later he was home. He stabled his mare, trudged to his apartment and set about making himself a late dinner. With another mug of decaffeinated coffee and a peanut butter sandwich in front of him, he bowed his head to give thanks. He found himself thanking *Gotte* for his sister and brother-in-law and their energetic group of *kinner.* He thanked the Lord for his food, and again he pictured Abigail's empty cupboard and stubborn expression.

And that was when he thanked *Gotte* for her spunk.

For the fact that her circumstances hadn't left her beaten, though she was obviously downtrodden.

For the amount in his savings account,

which allowed him to defer any wages she would owe him.

For their bishops who had kept an eye on her situation, even when she'd quite obviously refused help.

By the time he raised his head, it was past nine, and though he was terribly tired, he was also ravenous. He bit into his sandwich. The bread that Mary Lehman had given him was fresh baked, the peanut butter creamy and the jam homemade. He finished it quickly, then tackled the container of pasta salad she'd left in his refrigerator. Mary and John Lehman were *gut* friends.

His life was a *gut* life.

He rinsed his dishes, then prepared for bed. The morning would bring another day with plenty of work. He'd do what he'd always done.

Eat well.

Sleep well.

And then get to it.

Chapter Four

Abigail was not looking forward to visiting her bishop. Luke seemed to be a nice enough man, though she felt as if she barely knew him. He'd helped with the funeral, of course. He'd visited her several times since and offered various forms of assistance. She'd been morbidly embarrassed and determined to handle everything on her own.

Thomas was right, though—she couldn't handle everything on her own.

She needed help.

Thomas.

What was she going to do about Thomas?

When she had finished her first cup of

coffee and worked up the energy to look outside, she'd immediately seen him. He'd been harvesting in the fields with the same men who'd been there the day before. At least they looked like the same men. She couldn't really make them out from so far away.

She tidied up the kitchen and checked the small hand mirror to be sure she looked presentable. She couldn't wear the same dress as the day before. It was dirty and she wouldn't do laundry until Monday. She put on her other dress, the one that was decidedly too tight. How would she make it two more months? She'd have to hide inside for lack of clothing.

Abigail put the hand mirror in her dresser drawer, snagged her purse off the hook by the back door and, at the last second, stepped back inside to fetch the list she'd made at Thomas's insistence. Then she walked to the barn, again wearing Asher's shoes.

Thomas.

How early did the man arrive? And was

he going to be there every day? She was grateful for his help, for sure and certain, but in the last month she'd become used to being alone.

And look where that's landed you.

Why was it that she always heard her mother's voice in a chiding tone in her head? The woman hadn't been a shrew, only strict and reserved. Somewhat harsh, if Abigail were honest about it. She pushed the memories away.

Thomas must have jogged to the barn because he was harnessing Belle before Abigail could attempt to do it herself. "I wasn't sure how early you'd want to go," he admitted.

"Best to get it over with." She attempted to soften the harsh words with a smile, but it felt false and forced.

Thomas patted her clumsily on the shoulder, then stepped back and stuck his thumbs under his suspenders. His shirt was already stained with sweat, and he had a bit of hay in his hair. She fought the urge to brush it away.

"I guess I'll be seeing you." She didn't add that hopefully he would be gone by the time she returned. She supposed that was asking for too much. She wanted the man to work for free and not to be around—an impossibility if there ever was one.

"*Ya*, for sure. Take your time. We have a full day's work, so I'll be here to unharness Belle when you return."

She almost rolled her eyes.

She could unharness her own horse. Then the baby kicked, and she realized that maybe she couldn't—not now. But the baby would be born by Thanksgiving. Surely then she'd be able to go back to taking care of everyday chores herself.

Bishop Luke's farm was less than a ten-minute buggy ride from her place. She pulled into the yard and was surprised when Luke's oldest son appeared in front of her buggy before it had properly stopped. He held the door of the buggy as she clambered out, then said, "Your horse is a beauty."

"Thank you, Isaac." His name came to her in a flash, and he smiled down at her.

Like his father, Isaac was tall and thin. And unlike Thomas Albrecht, he didn't seem bothered by her large stomach. No doubt he remembered his *mamm* being in her last trimester. How many children did Luke and Naomi have? She should know since she'd been in the community for nearly a year now, but she hadn't become well acquainted with anyone yet. Plus, there were easily over a hundred children at their church services. It was difficult to tell who belonged to whom.

As she walked toward the front porch, she noticed two boys washing off the bishop's buggy. Another boy was brushing down a roan gelding, and two girls were beating rugs against the porch railing. They waved hello as she walked up, then ran inside to call their *mamm*.

Naomi pushed open the screen door, smiling and drying her hands on a dish towel. "Abigail, come on in. It's *gut* to see you. Would you like some tea?"

"Nein. Danki." Her stomach betrayed her and picked that moment to let out a growl. "Well, maybe tea would be *gut.*"

"And apple strudel. I loved apple strudel when I was pregnant. Unless you don't like apples."

"Sounds *gut,* actually."

So it was that she found herself sitting at the table, enjoying the freshly baked treat and tea when Luke walked in. Bishop Luke was quite tall and thin; whereas Naomi was his exact opposite. They should have made an odd couple, but instead they looked as if they'd been created for one another.

Luke sat across the table, but Naomi took the chair next to her.

"It's *gut* to see you, Abigail. *Wunderbaar* to see you out and about."

"Yes, well..." She stared down into her teacup for a moment, then raised her eyes to his. "The man you sent to help me— Thomas Albrecht—he has a convincing way about him."

"I've heard excellent things about Thomas. An Amish handyman of sorts."

"I suppose." Pressed to describe him, she would use words like stubborn and pushy and opinionated, but there was no need to bring that up now. She pulled her purse into her lap and retrieved the business card from her purse.

"I went to the bank yesterday and met with Mr. Webb." Neither Luke nor Naomi interrupted Abigail, so she continued. "My name isn't on the bank account. Also, Asher didn't have a will. The estate will have to be probated, and that could take some time."

She placed the card on the table and pushed it toward Luke.

"He suggested I hire this woman, but of course I have no money to do so." She quickly added, "I will, but at this point I'm not allowed to access what's in the bank account."

"I see." Luke tapped the card, then looked up and smiled at her. "Gabriela Martinez is well-known in our community. She's fair and familiar with our ways. Plus, her rates are reasonable."

"But I don't have any money to pay her, even if her rates are fair."

"Aaron Lapp is our deacon who handles such matters. I'll speak with him when I see him at our church service tomorrow. The benevolence fund has a healthy balance. He'll contact Ms. Martinez on Monday and arrange payment. You should call her and make an appointment."

"Okay. *Danki.*"

"We are happy to help in any way that we can, Abigail." Luke's words were soft, kind—not at all judgmental.

It was Naomi who prodded the conversation forward. "You'll need money to live on until this is settled."

Abigail nodded, the lump in her throat blocking any words.

"And how are you set for the *boppli*?"

She shook her head.

"Let me grab some paper and a pencil."

Abigail almost laughed at that, remembering the night before as well as the list in her purse. She didn't need to look at the list. The words, the horror of her situation, were seared into her brain and lay heavy on her heart.

"Thomas has taken care of your fields?" Luke asked.

"The men should be finished with the harvest today. There's still a lot of work to do, according to him, and he's offered to help around the place...for free until I can afford to pay him."

At this, the bishop's right eyebrow shot up, but he quickly hid his surprise and nodded. "Excellent. Things are shaping up. *Ya?*"

"I guess. It's all a bit...overwhelming."

"Of course it is." Naomi had sat back down, but when she saw the tears coursing down Abigail's cheeks, she hopped up and fetched a box of Kleenex.

Both the bishop and his wife waited until she'd calmed before saying anything else.

"I'm sorry," she mumbled.

"There is no need to apologize." Luke placed one hand over the other on the table.

They were a farmer's hands. Luke was a farmer like just about every other man in their Plain community. His life, his home, even his family was similar to theirs. He faced the same trials that they did, which caused them to believe that he understood their struggles as well as their joys. All of that helped them to receive the message he preached on Sundays. Now, sitting at his table, Abigail realized that perhaps he did understand the depth of her misery.

"*Gotte* has a plan for you, Abigail. A plan for you and your *boppli*, but the road we must travel can sometimes be difficult."

"Or impossible."

"No, my child. Never impossible." He waited until she once again looked at him. "People want to help, Abigail. Do you remember the other times I visited? The times you sent me away?"

Abigail nodded.

"I left without insisting because help has to be accepted. It can't be forced on someone, but Abigail…we would never have gone completely away. I would have continued to visit every week, because you're a part of our family."

Her tears started falling again. Abigail pulled another tissue from the box, wishing she could control her emotions better.

"It's a privilege for family members to help one another," Luke continued. "Paul wrote in Galatians that the entire law can be summed up in a single command—'love your neighbor as yourself.' You, Abigail, are giving others an opportunity to do that."

Then Luke closed his eyes and began to pray. He asked *Gotte* to bless Abigail and the baby, to grant wisdom to Gabriela Martinez, to give strength to Thomas Albrecht, and he thanked their Heavenly Father for allowing the congregation to minister to one of their own.

An hour later, Abigail made her way home, exhausted but also more at peace than she'd been since finding her husband dead in the barn. Thomas hurried from the field to help with Belle, releasing the mare into an adjacent pasture where he'd put his own horse. Apparently, the other men helping with the harvest had walked, so they must be nearby neighbors. How could she not know that? It was as if she'd been living in a bubble, and now that bubble had burst.

Belle practically pranced toward Thomas's mare, and then they were nosing one another like the oldest of friends.

"It's easy being a horse." Thomas peered into the back of her buggy. "Let me bring those bags in for you."

"Oh, I can handle them myself."

"Abigail, are you going to argue every time I try to help you?"

"I might if I can do it myself."

"Fine."

"Fine." She glowered at him, but Thomas didn't move. If she'd used such a perturbed tone with Asher, he would have stomped off and then given her the silent treatment for a week.

Thomas, on the other hand, looked as if he was about to start laughing. "I was the oldest of four. The other three were girls, so I'm pretty good at waiting on a woman."

"Are you, now?"

"Sure." He grinned, removed his hat and combed his fingers through his hair. "I've been well trained."

The last thing she wanted to do was stand in the yard and argue with this man. Plus, her feet were starting to swell again. Even in Asher's shoes, she could feel them growing more tender. "Since you're trained and stubborn, let's not waste our time. I'll take in one of the bags and you can grab the rest."

"*Gut* compromise."

There were three bags of clothing and a box of food. Abigail would have been embarrassed if she wasn't so very excited about having something to wear that would fit her. Since Naomi was the same height as Abigail, but quite a bit heavier, her clothes were about the right size. Apparently, whenever she sewed a new dress, which wasn't that often in an Amish home, she took the oldest, mended it and saved it for anyone in need.

Abigail was certainly in need.

How nice it would be to wear something that she wasn't afraid of busting at the seams.

She and Thomas carried everything into the kitchen.

"Should I...make you and the other men lunch?"

Thomas stared down into the box, shaking his head. "I think this food is for you, Abigail. Plus, we all brought our own lunch, but it was a nice offer."

"Okay."

"Okay."

"Well, *danki*."

"*Gem gschehne.*"

There it was again, the old words passing between them like a bubbling spring flowing over dry, parched land.

Why wasn't Thomas Albrecht married? She stood at the kitchen window, watching him join the men in the field, and pondered that question. She supposed she might never know, and did it really matter? She certainly wasn't in the market for a new spouse. *Nein*, marriage hadn't been a *gut* fit for her.

Perhaps she was too stubborn. She wasn't really sure why she'd never felt any real affection for Asher, nor he for her. Her marriage had been woefully missing warmth or kindness of any type. At first, she'd thought it was her fault, that she was somehow wanting in an area that mattered to Asher.

After six months of marriage, she learned that wasn't the case. Asher was stiff and distant around everyone—not that they had company often, but they had hosted church service twice. Fortunately, both of those times the weather had been nice enough to hold the service outside. There was no way their whole congregation could fit in their house, though they might have fit in the barn.

Perhaps Asher was an introvert. He'd been an only child, so it was possible he'd never grown used to being around others. Regardless, she knew six months into her marriage that being detached was simply his personality. It made living with him difficult for them both. Why had he wanted to marry? Asher was never comfortable around her, never relaxed in her presence. And he never, ever spoke kindly to her.

Neither had her *mamm*.

Or even her *dat*.

Perhaps she was unlovable.

"That's ridiculous," she scolded herself as she went about setting the food Naomi had sent into her refrigerator and in the pantry. "No thing that *Gotte* makes is unlovable, and you—Abigail Yutzy—are made by *Gotte*."

She almost laughed out loud. Apparently, the trip to the bishop's had helped her more than she realized. Or possibly it was the thought of the clothes waiting in the bags. Or the knowledge that women would gather at her house on Monday to help her prepare for the baby.

She still hadn't met with the lawyer.

She still didn't have any money.

But suddenly the day didn't seem so hopeless.

Meet with Gabriela Martinez. Settle

Asher's estate. Pay Thomas and send him on his way. In the meantime, keep her distance.

That was her plan, and she fully intended to see it through.

Thomas couldn't decide if Abigail looked bigger in the newer, roomier clothes, but she definitely looked more comfortable. She was sitting on the front porch, her feet up on a small stool that she'd fetched from the barn.

"We finished with the harvest." He stood at the bottom of the porch steps, slapping his hat against his pants leg. He was dirty and tired, but he was satisfied with what they'd accomplished. "If you'd like, I can ask in town to see how much money you can get for it."

Abigail blinked twice, then sat up straighter. "I hadn't thought of that."

"Selling the crop?"

"I mean… I know you sell crops. I am Amish, despite what you may think."

"Never said you weren't."

"I hadn't thought about the money. That will come in handy."

Thomas cleared his throat, waiting for Abigail to stop staring off into the distance. There were practically thought bubbles above her head of all she planned to purchase with the harvest money.

"Your horse needs some things for the winter."

"Things?"

"There's plenty of hay, but you'll need protein to supplement that."

"How much is—"

"Plus, you'll need the farrier to come by soon."

"I don't even know who that is."

"Can't say as I'm surprised. It doesn't seem like Belle's hooves have been attended to in a while. The last thing you need is a lame mare."

Abigail glowered at him, but did he back off? He did not, because although he was a patient person, he wasn't actually paying attention to the signals that Abigail was throwing his direction. He was tired and dirty and wanted to go home and shower.

"Then there's the goats in the back field that will also need winter supplies. And there is the cost of the cover crop, which we talked about on the first day I was here."

"Stop." Abigail slapped her hand against the arm of the rocker. "Do I look like I'm worried about a cover crop? Or goats? The only thing I'm worried about at this minute is this *boppli*."

Her hand rested on her stomach, and Thomas thought maybe he saw the unborn child move.

He stepped back.

"Maybe we shouldn't talk about this right now."

"Absolutely we're going to talk about it. Don't go figuring out how I'm going to spend money from a harvest that I didn't even know I'd receive."

He held up his hands and again stepped back. If she kept glaring at him, he'd end up in the field before she finished venting.

Abigail didn't appear to notice that he was retreating.

She lumbered to her feet and stepped closer. "Do you have any idea how long it's been since I had even ten dollars in the cash jar?"

"Abigail..."

"Over a month. That's how long. Because Asher died on a Sunday and he would put cash in the jar on Monday, so I could go to the store during the week. Of course, he couldn't a month ago because he was lying dead in the barn, where I found him."

She was now making her way down the steps, so Thomas took yet another step back.

"And why do you keep backing away from me as if I'm contagious?"

He held up his hands. "I never said you were contagious, but maybe you should..."

"Do *not* tell me to calm down, Thomas Albrecht. If you have any goodness at all in you, do not tell me to calm down. I have a child coming, and I am going to need money for that child."

"Your church—"

"I will not depend on the charity of my church if I can do it on my own."

"I wasn't suggesting—"

But it was obvious that Abigail wasn't listening. The goat had appeared and began to munch on her dead plants. Before Thomas could shoo the animal away, Abigail had snatched up the broom and was proceeding to thrust it at the goat, who continued to snatch away pieces of the dead plant, bleating at her between bites.

Instead of yielding, Abigail raised the broom and landed a good solid slap on the goat's rump, who looked at her once then darted away.

Thomas didn't know who was more surprised—him or the goat. He thought Abigail might start crying again.

Or perhaps holler at him more.

Instead, she sank to the porch steps and let out a howl of laughter. It was possibly more frightening than her tears.

He shuffled from one foot to the other.

Gingerly, he took the broom away and

placed it against the porch railing. Why was he always taking a broom away from her?

Unsure what else to do, he attempted to stick the now-decimated plant back into the pot.

Finally, Abigail wiped her eyes and pulled in a deep breath. "Naomi sent a loaf of pumpkin bread. Care for some?"

"Depends. Do I get to eat it? Or are you going to throw it at me?"

Instead of replying, she pulled herself up, climbed the steps and disappeared into the house. Thomas had no idea whether he should go in and help, so he swept the steps clean of the dirt caused by the goat's bad manners. He set the broom at the corner of the porch, looked around for something else to do and found nothing. Finally, he opened the front door and stuck his head inside. "Need help?"

"*Ya*. Please."

He found her in the kitchen, slicing pumpkin bread onto a plate. The kettle on the stove had begun to whistle, so he poured the hot water into the two mugs she'd set out, happy to see that her tea tin was once again full.

Abigail met his gaze. A tiny smile was all that remained of her giggling fit. "Outside or in?"

"It's nice on the porch."

"Outside it is." She grabbed a sweater from the back of a chair and slipped it around her shoulders. The color was a deep blue, and made her look all the prettier. He wondered if it had come from the bag of clothing. Did pregnant women need bigger sweaters as well as bigger dresses and shoes?

She picked up the plate of bread. He picked up the mugs and followed her outside.

He didn't feel as bad about eating her food or drinking her tea, since the bishop's wife had obviously sent a good deal of supplies home with her. He'd made it through his second piece of bread when she finally spoke.

"Have you ever been on an *Englisch* carnival ride?"

"Once." Thomas smiled at the memory. "Unfortunately, I'd had a corn dog, soda and cotton candy beforehand. Lost all of it the minute I stepped off the ride."

Abigail's head bobbed in agreement. "My parents would never allow such a waste of money, but I went with a friend once to a local fair. This was in Monte Vista, where I grew up."

"Colorado, right?"

"Yup. Small community. Anyway, they have this rodeo once a year, and my *mamm* was off at a relative's back east and my *dat* just wanted to be rid of me and my siblings for a few hours. No doubt, we were a handful."

He didn't interrupt. She seemed more relaxed than she had since he'd met her, though her expression was no longer smiling.

"Anyway. I didn't eat before the ride, didn't have any extra money at all, but my best friend purchased two ride tickets. The fair wasn't big enough to have an actual roller coaster, but there was this teacup thing."

"I remember that one." Thomas swirled his finger. "Round and round."

"Exactly. I tried to walk after we got off the ride, and I kept lurching side to side." She looked at him then, looked directly at him without the wall that normally seemed to separate her. "That's what my life feels like now. Like I'm lurching from side to side—one moment sad and crying and the next laughing hysterically. It's not…it's not proper. I'm sorry."

He met her gaze, looked so deeply into those brown eyes that he felt like he was falling. He gulped and glanced away. "You don't have to apologize, Abigail. You've suffered a tragedy with your husband's death, and now you're in a precarious situation and pregnant on top of that. It's hard on a person… I know because my *schweschder* has had six *bopplin* in six years."

"Oh my."

"Lily has a husband and a secure home,

and my other *schweschdern* close by, plus me." He shook his head. "Still, she has those ups and downs, or side to sides, or whatever you call them. I think it might be the baby hormones coupled with the lack of sleep."

"Six *bopplin*." She shook her head and rubbed her stomach at the same time. "I know Amish have big families, but I can't imagine dealing with six children. Honestly, I'm not sure how well I'll handle one."

"My other *schweschder* Grace has two, and my youngest *schweschder*, Lydia, is pregnant with her first." He broke off another piece of the pumpkin bread and popped it in his mouth. "What I'm saying is you don't have to apologize. I understand. Well, I mean I can't understand myself since I haven't experienced it, but I can guess what it's like."

She studied him a minute, and he wondered if she was about to lurch to one side or the other. But instead, she said, "You're a nice person, Thomas."

"*Danki.*"

"And I'll let you know by Monday what I plan to do with the harvest money." When he smiled, she added quickly, "Don't spend any of it. This is my decision, and I know those things you mentioned are important, but I need time to think about it."

"Fair enough, just don't—"

"Wait too long. *Ya.* I can see you're anxious to whip things into shape around here."

"It's what you're paying me to do."

That sat between them, the irony of it sharp and shiny. She wasn't actually paying him anything.

"I guess I should be going." He stood, then stopped to pick up the teacup and plate, but she waved him away.

"I'll take care of it."

He was being dismissed. The sun was setting on a beautiful Saturday, and moments ago he'd been itching to get home. Not now, though. Now he would have preferred rocking on Abigail's porch.

"Have a *gut* Sunday." He was down the

steps before he turned back to her. "My *bruder*-in-law needs some help Monday, so I won't be back until Tuesday. If that's okay."

"Tuesday will be fine."

Normally, he enjoyed rotating his job sites, but for some reason the thought of not seeing Abigail Yutzy for two days didn't sit right with him. What if she needed him? What if something went wrong on the farm? What if she couldn't get to a phone?

All of those worries were ridiculous.

He'd written the number to the mercantile on the pad she kept on the kitchen counter.

If something went wrong on the farm, she would call.

And if she couldn't get to a phone, she had the emergency bell hanging on the front porch. Her nearest neighbor would be there much faster than he could be.

Abigail Yutzy might be lurching from side to side as if she'd just stepped off an *Englisch* carnival ride, but emotionally speaking he suspected that she was a strong woman. At least he hoped she was.

The real problem was she didn't seem to realize that yet.

He thought again of his own mother. She was kind, but also emotionally weak and unable to cope with the trials of a drunken husband. Thomas had to take over the running of their farm at a young age, and his *schweschdern* had taken over the running of the house.

But Abigail wasn't his mother.

He thought of her brown eyes, of the way she'd covered her face when she'd been consumed by laughter, of her hands clasped around the teacup. Then, he remembered her insistence that she would decide how to spend the crop money. She was stubborn, but stubbornness could be a sign of strength.

She would recover her balance.

She'd learn to stand on her own two feet.

At least he hoped she would, for the sake of her and her unborn child.

Chapter Five

Abigail woke Monday morning with an unsettled feeling in her stomach. At first, she worried something was wrong with her *boppli*. Putting her hand to her stomach, she whispered, "Are you okay in there?"

The baby's only answer was a slight pushing against Abigail's left side, but it was answer enough.

It wasn't until she had donned her robe and padded to the bathroom that she remembered. Today was the day. She glanced at the clock. In two hours, she would be visited by the women from her church.

The day before had passed like most Sundays. The neighbor boy who was cleaning

Belle's stall had harnessed the horse for her. Nate was part of their east-side Plain community, and no doubt his parents had reminded him to harness the horse. Abigail was grateful that he had.

She had purposely arrived at the church meeting at the last possible moment. She dreaded the thought of standing around and making conversation. She wasn't good at that. She didn't know if she ever had been, but now—with her stomach as large as a beach ball and the fact that she was a widow—she had no idea what to say. And she didn't think she could abide the looks of pity.

Instead of dealing with that, she waited until the clock on the wall told her she might be late, clambered out to the buggy and drove through a day that threatened rain. Clouds pressed down—dark and gloomy. A wind from the north made it feel more like October than September. She didn't mind—not really. Cold weather meant she was even closer to the birth of her child.

A teenage boy was there to take her horse and buggy. She hurried inside, depositing her plate of oatmeal cookies on the dessert table, then slipping into a back bench on the women's side. Once the service was over, she made her way to help at the serving line, but all of the women shooed her away.

"You get a pass once you hit the last trimester," Naomi explained. "Go and rest your feet."

So, she did, and people were polite to her. The problem was that she didn't really know them. When they smiled at her, then quickly looked off, she couldn't say if it was from embarrassment for her and her situation or simply because they had a wayward child they needed to keep an eye on. That was the problem with being around other people. How could you ever really know what they were thinking?

A few of the women stopped by and said they were looking forward to seeing her the next day. Abigail thanked them, ate as quickly as possible and then excused herself and hurried home. No one questioned her leaving early.

She sat at the kitchen table Monday morning, grateful that the rain was holding off. She didn't want Naomi to have to get out in the rain because of her.

Then her thoughts drifted back to the day before and how awkward it had been. It was her first time back at the church meeting since Asher had died. Perhaps in the last month she'd forgotten how to act around others. She'd been shy before, but never socially awkward. That had developed after her marriage. The question confronting Abigail as she rinsed out her breakfast dishes and hurried to dress was whether she wanted to stay that way.

If she didn't, what was she willing to do about it?

Instead of trying to figure out her own personality, she dressed and set about making the house look hospitable. She put coffee mugs out on the counter and opened the tea tin, making sure it was full. She filled the teakettle with water and set it on the stove.

How many women should she expect? Three? Four?

She fluffed the pillows on the couch, then proceeded to remove the piles of junk mail and old newspapers and tossed clothing. Both chairs in the living room needed straightening. How did furniture move when she was the only one in the house?

Then there was the dust. It was settled so thick upon the shelves that she could have written "Welcome" there. Instead, she fetched a rag and a can of furniture polish. At least it gave the room a fresh smell, though if anyone bothered to check under the furniture for dust bunnies, they were apt to find several.

She tried to convince herself it didn't matter.

But she was a bit aghast at how much she'd let things go. No wonder Thomas had told her to stop crying. He'd walked through her living room. No doubt his bachelor pad was cleaner than her place.

What had she been doing since Asher's death other than wringing her hands and worrying? Before she could settle on a good answer to that question, the buggies started arriving. Abigail stepped out onto the porch. Her mouth fell open. She snapped it shut and pressed her fingers to her lips. She couldn't believe what she was seeing. For a moment, all of her worries fled. All of these women were coming to see her?

The scene in front of her reminded Abigail of the day of Asher's funeral. Only today, instead of solemn families reminding *kinder* to be quiet and respectful, there were *mamms* and *bopplin* and laughter and smiles.

Soon her living room was filled with women, some holding infants, others shooing young children off to the front porch or the backyard. School was in session, so there was a plethora of small children and the occasional teenage girl who had already graduated from eighth grade. The boys were probably home helping their *dat*, but the girls were here and proceeded to herd their siblings.

"It's a beautiful day," Naomi told her youngest.

"There's a storm coming."

"Not in the next hour. Now go and play outside, but stay close to the house."

The names fell around her like red and yellow and orange leaves falling to the ground—Mary and Deborah and Clare and Elizabeth. For the first time since moving to Shipshe, Abigail felt herself to be a part of the group.

It felt like being held by her *grossmammi*.

Before she could analyze that comparison, her eyes drifted to the things they had brought. Onesies in all colors, tiny T-shirts, small dresses if her baby was a girl and pants with matching shirts if it was a boy. Sweaters that had been crocheted and knitted in yellow and green and pink and blue. The gifts were piled on the coffee table, unwrapped, of course. Plain folk didn't bother with wrapping paper and bows, but oh, how the gifts lifted Abigail's spirit. And some were tied with bits of ribbon that she'd save to put in her *doschder*'s hair or use to amuse her son.

"Whichever clothes you don't use, you can take to the next baby shower," Clare explained. She wore a dark green dress and looked to be Abigail's age. She had blond hair to Abigail's brown, was a good three inches taller and thin as a whip. She also seemed quite nice. "Better to have it on hand and need it, than need it and not have it."

Several times Abigail blinked away tears.

Her fingers brushed against the knitted blankets and crocheted caps. Then two teenage girls carried in a bassinet and two other girls stood in the doorway holding what looked like the mattress for a cradle.

"Do you want the bassinet in your room?"

"*Ya*. Please. I'll show you where." She peeked into the bassinet, made of a beautiful oak and shined to perfection. Inside were sheets, more blankets, and several stacks of cloth diapers along with a large jar of diaper pins.

The girls set the bassinet within arm's reach of Abigail's bed. She stood there, staring down at it, when she realized that someone was waiting for her at the door. Clare motioned the girls back into the hall and joined Abigail near the bassinet.

"It's all a bit overwhelming," Abigail admitted.

"I'm sure it is. Just remember that you still have some time. The *boppli* won't be born for a while yet. Right?"

"My due date is near Thanksgiving."

"*Gut.* The girls have a crib to bring in too. It's been taken apart, of course, since we brought it in the buggy. I can send my husband over to put it together for you."

"Thomas can do it." The words popped out of her mouth before she even considered them.

"The Amish property manager, right?" Clare's eyes practically danced. "Strange occupation for a Plain person, but I heard he's *gut* at it."

"I guess." He was excellent at it—other than the fact that he was pushy and stubborn and opinionated. Three reasons she didn't want to go into that particular topic of conversation.

"If you decide you want the bassinet or the crib in a different place, you have time to move it—or you have time to ask Thomas to move it. I do not suggest you try to do so yourself." She cocked her head to the side. "I'm Clare, by the way. It can be hard to remember everyone's name."

Tears stung Abigail's eyes. Why was it that she always felt so inadequate? "I've lived here nearly a year. I should... I should have tried to reach out more."

"It's been a difficult time, *ya*?"

Abigail nodded and swiped at her eyes.

Clare picked up one of the cloth diapers and handed it to her. "*Gut* for diapers, burp rags or drying tears."

Abigail thanked her and blotted her eyes, hoping everyone in the living room wouldn't be able to tell that she'd been weeping.

"Now…where do you want the baby crib? With my son I put it in the corner of the room, but with my daughter I wanted it across from the window."

"You have two children?"

"Justin is three, and Melody turned one last month. Their cousin has them both outside at the moment. My next is due in the spring."

"You're…" Abigail glanced down at Clare's stomach, which had the smallest swell to it.

"I am. You know how Amish are—lots of babies."

Abigail laughed. It sounded foreign to her own ears, but it felt just right.

"Back to the crib—I usually have my husband move it to several different places. I can't really tell until I see it. Do you know what I mean?" Clare smiled with a twinkle in her eyes. Someone with a sense of humor was exactly what Abigail needed.

"I haven't given it much thought. I mean, I have, but I didn't have any furniture so it was rather a moot point."

"Well, you won't want the baby in your room much past the first couple of months. Do you plan to set up a nursery?"

Abigail bit her bottom lip. Yes, she'd planned to, but she hadn't known how to begin. Then there was the problem of Asher's study. What was she to do with all of the stuff piled in the room? Their home only had the two bedrooms, though of course Asher had big plans for adding more rooms when they had more children. One thing Asher had never been short of was plans.

"Could we just leave it in the living room for now?"

"Of course we can. It's your home. You set things up where you want them." Clare's tone was soothing, kind even.

She waited until Abigail nodded, then instructed the girls to set the mattress and side boards in the living room next to the couch. It would make for a tight fit, but Abigail would deal with furniture arranging later.

She'd thought the women would come,

offer their gifts, have a cup of tea and then leave. Instead, they reached into their large shoulder bags or bulky diaper bags and pulled out knitting or crocheting or even darning work.

After they'd been stitching and talking and laughing for nearly an hour, several women set their sleeping babes on a blanket on the floor. It was that sight that touched Abigail more than anything else. Those girls and boys would be her baby's classmates and best friends.

It brought a lump to her throat to think of that. They would make up the community that her child would grow up in, and Abigail was determined that her child would feel at home and safe and happy. If there was anything she could do to make that true, then she would do it.

If the lawyer could deal with probating Asher's estate.

If she was allowed to keep the farm.

If there was enough income from the crops to allow her to survive there.

Too many ifs.

Too many questions she couldn't begin to answer.

As her energy flagged, she felt overwhelmed by them.

It was Naomi who noticed the shift in Abigail's mood. She cleared her throat and stuffed her knitting back into her bag. Then she sat up straighter and raised a hand to catch everyone's attention. Soon the other women followed suit until the room was silent except for the soft snoring of babies inside and the cheerful sounds of children playing outside.

"Abigail, we are happy to share from our abundance, to supply you with the things you need for the child that will soon arrive."

There were murmurs of "Amen" and "Yes" and "*Gotte* bless Abigail's child."

"But what we have to give is more than things. We also offer you our friendship. We are here for you whenever you need us—when you're frightened and don't know if a fever is due to teething or something more serious. When you've walked the floor but can't find a way to settle your child's tummy. When you spill the milk and misplace the pacifier and burn the dinner."

Laughter rolled around the circle, but Naomi's voice grew suddenly serious.

"Or when you are crying and need a shoulder. When you wish for someone to watch your *boppli* so you can nap. When you are lonely and need someone to simply sit with you and share a cup of tea." Naomi smiled and waited for Abigail to meet her eyes. Then she said, "We are here for you, Abigail. We are your family."

"Danki." That one word was so woefully inadequate, but Abigail didn't trust herself to say more.

Apparently, it was all they needed to hear, for Naomi smiled broadly and said, "Ladies, let's pray."

The prayer felt like the gentlest of rains, soaking into Abigail's parched soul. Then there was a blur of activity as everyone gathered their items and children. Each woman paused to speak with her before leaving. It wasn't until the last buggy had trundled down the lane and Abigail had returned inside that she found the stack of cards on her kitchen table. She wanted nothing more than to lie down and sleep for hours, but she didn't do that. Her curiosity wouldn't allow her to. So instead of napping, she made herself another cup of herbal tea, sat down at the table and began to read.

Each card had a handwritten message containing a recipe, or advice for a newborn, or a handwritten pattern for knitting or crocheting. All had a signature and phone number of the nearest phone shack or a business phone at the bottom.

Could it possibly be this easy?

Had Abigail's isolation and loneliness this past year been her own fault? Had these ladies simply been waiting for her to be approachable?

And now, in her time of need, they had come.

Abigail carefully restacked the cards, then tied them with a bit of ribbon. She would keep them. She'd read them when she was blue, and if she needed to, she would call on first one and then another. Because the one thing she knew for certain was that she couldn't do this alone.

And there was no reason for her to even try.

She should have slept well that night, but she woke after only an hour, the loneliness causing an ache in her heart that stole her breath.

She'd dreamed of Asher, turning away.

She'd dreamed of Thomas, waiting patiently for her to calm.

She'd dreamed of her parents.

Abigail's heart was flooded with the fear that she had no one. Her *bruders* and *schweschdern* were scattered about in different Amish communities. Everyone who was old enough to move away had done so. Her two youngest *schweschdern* had yet to marry and still lived at home. But Abigail wasn't welcome in her parents' home. She'd actually brought it up in a phone call with her *mamm*. Abigail had hinted she might move back. Her *mamm* had scoffed at the idea. "Your home is there, Abigail. It's best you learn to accept that."

But her home wasn't really here. She didn't even own this place—not yet. And Asher had no family. Didn't her *mamm* realize how alone she was? How lonely she was? Since she was a teenager, she had worried that her *mamm* didn't care, though it was possible that she did care but didn't know how to express it.

As the clock ticked toward three in the morning, Abigail felt more alone than she ever had, even more so than that first night after Asher's death. The ache seemed to reside deep in her bones, so deep that she had no tears for it.

She, Abigail Yutzy, was alone.

Best you learn to accept that.

The women who had visited her had been kind, and she thought real friendships might grow from the sympathetic group. But she needed to remember that each of them had families of their own—children and a husband.

She, on the other hand, had no one.

* * *

Thomas arrived a bit later than usual on Tuesday morning. He'd been helping his *bruders*-in-law put in their cover crop the day before, so he hadn't made it into town as he'd planned. Instead, bright and early on Tuesday he drove into town, checked on the price he could get for Abigail's crop, then directed Duchess to Abigail's house.

He was pleased with the price quoted.

It was possible the money would be enough to purchase the items he'd mentioned as well as leave a bit for Abigail to get by on. He wondered if she'd heard anything from the attorney yet.

But when he pulled down the drive, all of those thoughts fled. Abigail was standing on the front porch and around her was a mound of…stuff. He could hardly make out what it all was. And why was it on her front porch?

Instead of going to the barn, he pulled up in front of the house. He had to hold back his laughter when he saw that she was wearing not only Asher's shoes, but also a pair of his pants, one of his shirts and even a pair of his suspenders to keep it all up. From a distance, she looked like Round John over in Middlebury. Wisely, he didn't mention that.

"Morning, Abigail." He hopped out of the buggy and walked up the porch steps.

"Thomas." She swiped at a lock of brown hair that had escaped her *kapp*.

"Problem?"

"Oh, I don't know." She put her hands on her hips.

If she'd slipped her thumbs under her suspenders, he wouldn't have been able to hold in the laughter. As it was, he clenched his jaw and looked away until he had his amusement under control.

"Can I help?"

"Well. Maybe." She finally looked at him. "If you have time."

"*Ya.* Um…should I put Duchess in the field, or do you think I might need the buggy to move some of this stuff?" Now that he was standing closer, he could see that there were tall stacks of newspapers and magazines, plus boxes of items that contained who-knew-what.

"I suppose a wheelbarrow would probably come in handy, but I don't think we need Duchess."

"Back in a flash, then." He climbed into the buggy, drove to the barn and unharnessed his horse. By the time he'd pushed the wheelbarrow to the porch, Abigail was holding the small of her back.

"You okay?"

"Sure, *ya*."

But when he climbed the step, he noticed that she had dark circles under her eyes and her gaze kept flicking back and forth between him, the stacks of stuff and the barn.

"Do we have a burn pile back there? I'd love to just burn all this stuff."

"Oh." He walked over to an open box, picked up the top item, which was a seed catalog from three years earlier, then tossed it back in the box. "I might have a better idea…"

But Abigail didn't seem to be listening.

Her eyes widened, and her hand went to her belly.

He straightened in alarm. "Say, you don't look so *gut*."

"Thanks, Thomas." Her tone was joking, but she couldn't quite meet his gaze. With both hands on her belly, she stared at the porch's floor—as if she was listening, as if the child were somehow speaking to her.

"Maybe I should go and fetch Naomi." Or someone, anyone who would know what to do because Thomas was seriously out of his comfort zone here.

"Nein."

"Nein. That's it?"

She offered him a weak smile. "They're fake contractions."

"How do you know they're fake?"

The morning was cool, the clouds still threatening, but sweat slipped down the back of his neck. The last thing he wanted to do was be here when Abigail went into labor. He was afraid to hold his own nephew. He couldn't imagine being trusted with a newborn, let alone delivering one. "I could go and call the hospital."

Abigail shook her head, sat in the rocker and blew out a deep breath. "Give me a minute. It will pass."

He stared at her in amazement. How could she be so calm? Wasn't she worried? Wasn't she scared?

"Water might be *gut*."

"*Ya*. Sure. Absolutely." He hurried inside and fetched a glass of water. By the time he'd returned to the porch, she looked markedly better.

"Fake contractions?"

"Yup."

"You're sure?"

"I'm sure. They've stopped. Braxton-Hicks contractions don't last long, and they don't get stronger."

"I've never heard of that."

"Oh, you will. When you have a *fraa* of your own and are expecting your first *boppli*, you'll hear all about it."

He didn't think so, but there was no need to go into that particular discussion now.

"How do you know all that stuff? I mean, this is your first, so how do you know what Brack-Holly…"

"Braxton-Hicks."

"Yes, those. How do you know what they are?"

"The doctor gave me a brochure. I've studied it top to bottom."

"Whew." He took off his hat and fanned his face. "You gave me quite the scare. Say, you're going to need someone to stay out here with you when you get closer to your date."

She waved away his concern. "I'm not worried about that today. I'm worried about all this…stuff."

"What is all this?"

"Asher's reading material, I guess."

"That would be a lot of reading."

"He never wanted to throw anything out. Said he might need it one day."

Thomas poked around in another box. "These seed catalogs are several years old. They wouldn't be much *gut* to anyone. Prices would be outdated, and the company might have even changed what they carry. I can see why you'd want to get rid of it, but why now? Why today?"

Instead of answering, Abigail chewed on her thumbnail. Finally, she met his gaze, stood and motioned him inside. He took one look around the living room and let out a long low whistle.

"I've never seen a crib next to a couch before. If that even is a crib. Why isn't it put together?"

"Because the husband usually does that."

"Oh. Right." He didn't mention the stack of baby things on the coffee table that was about to tip over. Apparently, the women of the church had come by and left Abigail with enough clothing and supplies for several newborns.

"Most people don't put their crib in the living room. Most people have a nursery." She scowled at him, then turned and walked down the hall, motioning for him to follow.

Though Asher had spent a lot of money on fancy fencing for horses he didn't yet own, he hadn't spent much on his house. It was surprisingly small. Thomas had only been in the living room and the kitchen, but he could tell from looking at the outside that it was what they called a starter home. Most houses were built small, then added to when they needed to accommodate a growing young family. Apparently, Asher hadn't yet shifted his priorities from the horses to the child.

"We only have the two bedrooms. Mine…" She hooked a thumb across the hall. "And this one—Asher's study."

"Asher had a study?"

"*Ya.* When I first married him, it didn't seem so odd." She walked into the room and trailed a hand across the dust on an old desk. "After all, he was a single man living alone. It made sense that he would have his office here instead of…"

"Instead of in the barn where most men keep this sort of thing." He picked up a broken harness that sat next to a can of oil. "Why would he do this kind of work in the house?"

Abigail shrugged. "I don't know. There were a lot of things about my husband that I didn't understand."

She bit her lower lip, and Thomas worried the waterworks were going to come on again. But instead, Abigail shook her head and rubbed at the back of her neck. "He was a *gut* man in his own way. He provided well for me."

Provided maybe, but definitely didn't prepare. Thomas didn't voice the uncharitable thought.

"I want this room to be my nursery. The living room is…"

"Crowded."

She laughed. "*Ya*. It is."

"The barn is fairly roomy."

"Why would I put my *boppli* in the barn?"

Thomas laughed. "I was thinking that I could clean out a corner, and we can put this desk and chair…and this halter…we can put it all out there. I don't think these are things you'll be needing anytime soon."

"And the boxes of outdated newspaper and magazines?"

"Shipshe has a recycling center. We can even get a penny a pound for what we take there."

"You don't say?"

"If we fill up the buggy, we should have enough for a pretzel at JoJo's."

They spent the rest of the morning on the project. By the time they'd cleared out the room and moved the boxes off the porch, Thomas's stomach was making loud grumbling sounds. Abigail slipped into the kitchen and made sandwiches. They ate them on the front porch as the sky darkened and the wind shifted.

"Cold front coming." Thomas didn't know why people tended to talk about the weather when they didn't know what else to say. Maybe it was simply a safe topic. He'd never made a woman cry discussing the weather. Come to think of it, he'd never made a woman cry before Abigail, and he couldn't say that he was the reason that she often ended up in tears. Perhaps it was her personality, or maybe it was the baby hormones. He'd heard about those from his *schweschdern.*

"The long dreary winter begins."

"You'll have a newborn baby. Trust me, you won't even notice the weather you'll be so tired."

"You and your words of encouragement."

He laughed, then told her how much money she could expect for the crop he'd harvested.

"That much?"

"*Ya.* I'm thinking I would only need half of it for the things I mentioned."

"That's *gut.* I guess. Is a cover crop really necessary?"

"It is. Keeps the soil in the ground, plus it provides nutrients for the crop we'll plant in the spring."

Abigail stifled a yawn.

"Don't let me keep you awake, though you did ask."

"Uh-huh. Say, any chance I could ride into town with you? Do you think the storm will hold off?"

"I do, and of course you can ride with

me. We're done loading the boxes. Anywhere in particular you need to go?"

"I spoke with Gabriela Martinez on the phone. She's going to handle the probate of the estate, but she left some papers at the front desk for me to sign. Her office is on the same road as Davis Mercantile."

"And the mercantile houses JoJo's. Sounds to me like we have a busy afternoon ahead."

An hour later, they'd delivered the old magazines to the recycling center, which had netted just under twelve dollars. It wasn't much, but on the other hand, he hadn't had to spend hours trying to burn the newspapers and magazines in a bonfire. It was while they were passing the hardware store that an idea struck him.

"Do you mind if we stop for a minute?"

"At the hardware store? Sure. I'll just wait here."

"*Nein.* I want you to come in with me." He led her to the paint aisle. "It seemed to me that your new nursery could use a fresh coat of paint. What color would you like it to be?"

Her face had taken on a thoughtful expression. "Paint would certainly help a lot, but I don't know if I'm up to painting an entire room."

He moved next to her and handed her a paint chip of a buttery yellow. "I'll paint the room, Abigail."

She glanced up at him, and he thought that she would argue, but instead a smile spread across her face.

He had the irrational thought that she was going to stand on tiptoe and kiss his cheek. Instead, she thrust the paint chip back at him. "This one, then. I love this one. And some white for the trim."

She would have used the last of the grocery money the bishop had given her to pay for the paint, but then the clerk said, "Want me to put it on your tab, Thomas?"

"That would be *gut*."

They walked back outside to a light drizzle.

"I guess we didn't beat the storm."

"Rain will be *gut* for the fields."

"For the cover crop?"

He nodded. "Once I get it planted."

Thomas turned to look at her and felt his breath catch in his throat. She'd turned her face up to his. A smile danced across her expression, and she had a healthy glow—she had a maternal glow.

He swallowed the lump and stepped back, bumping into the buggy.

"Something wrong?"

"Nein."

"You looked like you'd had a fright."

"No. Uh-uh. Nothing to be afraid of. I was just…um…looking at the window displays—nice fall stuff."

"Didn't guess you to be a window-display kind of guy." When they climbed back into the buggy, she teased him. "You have a tab? You must be a well-known handyman around this town."

"Oh, I am. Folks line up for miles to beg me to work for them."

The laughter felt good, so much better than the look of despair on her face that he'd seen when he first arrived that morning. The day wasn't going at all like he'd planned. He'd meant to harvest the back garden of any remaining vegetables and then check the north fence. But what were those things when compared to preparing a nursery for a soon-to-arrive *boppli*?

And before they did that, they needed to go to the attorney's office so Abigail could sign her papers. Then one last stop by Jo-Jo's for one of her famous pretzels and a cup of coffee or hot chocolate. Thomas had the distinct feeling that though Abigail had lived in Shipshe for nearly a year, she didn't yet know the place. She didn't really appreciate all the little community had to offer.

And JoJo's Pretzels? It was a fine place to start.

Not that he was getting involved.

He'd had several stern talks with himself about that the day before. He'd even forgotten what he was doing a couple of times and found himself plowing a row he'd already plowed. The guys had teased him about that. But he'd straightened his head out regarding Abigail.

They'd be friends. He'd see that she was on her feet before he moved on to the next job. Might be a few months, but it wasn't going to be years. That was a worst-case scenario.

Because spending a couple of years with Abigail would not be prudent. He was strong and stern with himself, but he was still a man. And she was a beautiful woman. Hopefully, within a few months the estate would be settled, she could hire permanent workers and he would be on his merry way.

Except suddenly, that didn't sound as appealing as it usually did.

And the thought that kept tumbling through his mind was *Yeah, I'll be on my way. But on my way to where?*

Chapter Six

Abigail was stunned at how quickly the next two weeks flew by. Thomas painted the *boppli*'s room and moved the crib into it. He spotted a changing table at a garage sale, cleaned it up and placed it in the room as well.

Abigail stood in the doorway of the room, looking at the freshly painted walls, crib with sheets that sported puppies and kittens, and the changing table that Thomas had carried in that morning.

Thomas.

What was she going to do about him?

He continued to have new ideas for the farm. Every single day, he'd stop inside after he'd finished his work. Every single time, they were less than five minutes into the conversation when he'd say, "I had an idea for..."

The man could not let things be for five minutes.

She admired his enthusiasm. And how could she complain? He was still working for free. Gabriela Martinez had filed the estate probate papers, but she had warned Abigail that the process was slow. "Best to prepare yourself for it to take a year, even eighteen months. If it's less, we'll celebrate."

Gabriela had also filed an emergency petition requesting that Abigail be allowed to use the funds in the bank account. She hoped to receive a ruling on that within seven to fourteen days.

The days of September had given way to October, the temperature had grown cooler, and much-needed rain began to fall each day. Abigail should have felt more optimistic, more encouraged, but each day became a little harder than the one before it. Even with the prospect of having a little more cash, Abigail didn't feel much like celebrating.

Her head ached, and she felt sick to her stomach.

Instead of folding the laundry that she'd managed to fetch from the line, she sat on the couch and closed her eyes. A soft rain had begun to fall outside, and the temperature had remained in the fifties—cold and dreary. It fit her mood. She slipped off her shoes and propped her feet up on the couch. She must have fallen asleep, because the next thing she knew Thomas was squatting in front of her attempting to wake her.

Abigail sat up straighter and tried to shake away the cobwebs. "What time is it?"

"Nearly five."

She sat forward, holding her head in her hands, trying to steel herself against the throbbing pain.

"What's wrong, Abigail?"

"My head."

"You have a headache?"

She closed her eyes, trying to form the words to explain that this was more than a headache, but found she was unable to do so.

Thomas let out a long, low whistle.

She opened one eye.

"What happened to your ankles?"

She glanced down, then closed her eyes again. "Swollen, I guess."

"That's more than swollen." He sat beside her on the couch. "I think I should call Naomi."

She tried to answer, and that was when the little food that she'd thought to eat that day made its way back up. Thomas just managed to grab a small trash can she kept under the end table and place it in front of her.

He patted her awkwardly on the back as she heaved again and again. When they were both quite sure she was done, he carried the trash can out of the room. She heard him go out to the mudroom. Then she heard him in the kitchen, filling a glass with water. He returned with the glass and a hand towel.

"Danki," she managed to say weakly. She took a sip from the glass and wiped at her mouth with the hand towel. Finally, she slid back down into a reclining position and curled into a ball. The room looked blurry, so she squeezed her eyes shut.

"I'm going to get the buggy. Don't... don't go anywhere."

"Couldn't if I wanted to."

She was vaguely aware of him hovering over her, covering her with a blanket from the back of the couch, then hurrying out the door. He returned, picked her up and carried her to the waiting buggy. She wanted to assure him that she could walk, but her head hurt so badly that the thought of forming words seemed impossible.

Instead, she rested her head against his shoulder.

Huddled against him.

Took comfort in his strength and the fact that he was there, that he cared, that he was willing to help her.

She thought the jostling of the buggy might bring more pain, but instead she found it was strangely comforting. If there was anything more soothing than the clip-clop of a horse, she didn't know what it was, and she was vaguely aware that Thomas's buggy had a heater.

She sat with her cheek resting against the buggy door, her eyes again closed. He'd brought the blanket from the couch— its weight and warmth seemed to assure her she would be okay. Only, she didn't feel okay. Something was wrong, but she didn't know what. Had she caught a stomach bug? Did she have the flu? Was her baby at risk?

Tears slipped down her cheeks as a soft rain pattered against the roof of the buggy and the last of the day's light faded to darkness.

They must have stopped at the bishop's, because suddenly Naomi was in the buggy, asking her questions about how long she'd felt this way and if there were labor pains.

Then Naomi was gone, and Abigail heard

her speaking to Thomas. "Take her to the hospital. Luke is late returning home from his weekly visit to ill church members. As soon as he arrives, we'll follow you."

And then there was the clip-clop of Duchess's hooves again. What a fine name for a horse—Duchess. Perhaps the mare came from a royal bloodline. Maybe Thomas was actually a prince. An Amish prince—now, that would be something. She thought she heard Thomas speak to her, then realized he was praying. And that was her last clear thought before she slipped into a troubled sleep, the pain finally receding.

The bright lights of the emergency parking area woke her. A nurse and orderly helped her out of the buggy. Thomas was attempting to answer their questions, and then they whisked her away. More questions followed as a blood pressure cuff was slipped over her arm and a baby monitor fastened around her belly. She was aware of the nurse calling out numbers and tsking and paging a doctor.

Abigail began to shiver, and the nurse put a heated blanket on her. She wanted to burrow into that blanket, that warmth. It reminded her of sunny summer days. It reminded her of Thomas's arms.

The doctor walked into the room and Abigail struggled to sit up and focus on her. She was middle-aged with short black hair and a kind smile.

"Mrs. Yutzy, my name is Dr. Rainey. Can you tell me how you're feeling?"

"I have a headache."

"That's from your blood pressure. It's quite high."

"Do I have the flu?"

"No. There's no fever or congestion, so it's doubtful you have the flu. I believe you have preeclampsia, but we're going to run a blood test and a urine test to confirm. I've ordered meds through your IV that should help ease your headache."

"What about my *boppli*?" Tears burned her throat, slid down her cheeks. "Is everything okay?"

"We're hearing a nice strong heartbeat.

Your baby is fine. It's good that you got in here as fast as you did. Preeclampsia can be quite dangerous if untreated. We'll also do an ultrasound just to be sure everything is fine." She smiled at Abigail and patted her arm.

Abigail was still worried. She felt terrible, but something about the woman's demeanor put her at ease.

"I'll be back to check on you in a few minutes."

She would have liked to sleep, but the nurses had other ideas in mind. They proceeded to gather urine and blood samples, and even brought in a portable sonogram machine. The doctor returned, squirted a cold gel on her belly and then ran a thing that looked like a spatula back and forth.

Then she heard it—the sound of her child's heartbeat. It was fast and steady and strong.

The doctor pointed at the monitor. "See? That's your baby."

"Where?"

"Here. You can see the head, and the

legs, and it looks like this one is a thumb-sucker."

Abigail stared at the screen as if it displayed her future, which it did. That was her baby? Inside of her? She stared until the picture began to make sense, until she could distinguish between the background and the child.

The doctor murmured that she'd be back in a few minutes, and the nurses returned. They cleaned the gel off her stomach, coaxed her into eating some Jell-O and pushed medication through her IV.

The headache became a distant memory.

The nausea vanished.

By the time Naomi stuck her head in the door, Abigail was starting to feel like her old self.

"Tell me everything," Naomi said, pulling a chair closer and perching on the edge of it. "You look better than you did at my house."

"I barely remember that."

"Preeclampsia?"

"*Ya.* How did you know?"

"We have a lot of *bopplin* born in our community. It's something that happens occasionally."

"The doctor assures me my *boppli* is fine."

"Oh, *ya*. I'm sure he or she is. You'll have to take it easy, Abigail. You'll need bed rest."

"It's not as if I do that much now." Abigail couldn't imagine doing less. It seemed that Thomas took care of nearly everything that needed to be done.

"You're still doing your laundry—washing it, hanging it on the line, fetching and folding it?"

"Of course."

"We'll have one of the teen girls come over to take care of that once a week. What about cleaning? Are you still doing that?"

"There's not that much to do, since there's only me."

"Sweeping and mopping?"

"Of course."

"Cooking?"

"A person has to eat." She plucked at the

bedcover. "I can't ask Thomas to do any more, Naomi."

"Thomas is happy to help you in any way he can." She sat back and folded her hands over her purse. "He was quite worried about you."

Abigail thought of his arms around her as he carried her to the buggy. She remembered the way it had felt to rest against his chest, the peace of allowing someone else to care for her. She shook the memory away and attempted to sit up straighter. "He's been a *gut* worker," she admitted. "I appreciate all he's done."

"He's more than a worker. He's your friend, and a person can never have too many of those. Don't you agree?"

"I suppose."

Dr. Rainey chose that moment to come into the room. Naomi stood to leave, but Abigail stopped her. "Stay, please. If it's okay..." She looked to the doctor, who nodded.

"Your preliminary test results are back, indicating a high level of protein in your urine as well as a low platelet count. Given the headache, the swelling…"

Dr. Rainey raised the blanket to take a peek at her legs. They all stared at her ankles, which resembled a picture she'd once seen of an elephant's legs.

"Already they're better than when you came in." Dr. Rainey cleared her throat and continued. "Given those things, as well as your high blood pressure, I'd say we have a fairly typical case of preeclampsia."

"But the *boppli* is fine?"

"Yes. Your baby is doing well. Would you like to know the sex?"

Abigail's eyes widened. Of course, she'd known that *Englischers* often had sonograms to find out such things. They even had gender reveal parties—which sounded both ridiculous and fun at the same time. It wasn't the Amish way. Amish tended to wait and see whether *Gotte* was blessing them with a boy or a girl.

She looked at Naomi, who shrugged and smiled mischievously. "The doctor apparently knows already. Do you want to know?"

"I do."

Dr. Rainey smiled. "Congratulations, then. You're having a baby girl."

At those words, a tenderness blossomed in Abigail's heart that she couldn't have imagined in her wildest dreams.

A baby girl. She was having a baby girl.

Naomi murmured, "*Gotte* is *gut*," and the doctor smiled broadly.

"That's…it's *wunderbaar*." Abigail swiped again at her tears. Why was she always crying? But these were tears of happiness. She was having a *doschder*. Warmth radiated through her body, and her hands went to her stomach, to her child, her little girl.

"Now, let's discuss your preeclampsia. I'm going to prescribe complete bed rest. I want you to lie on your left side as much as possible, and I'll send a prescription for medicine to lower your blood pressure."

"Okay. Um…bed rest for how long?"

The doctor exchanged a look with Naomi,

and Abigail knew she wasn't going to like the answer.

Dr. Rainey set her tablet down on the counter and snagged the rolling stool the nurse had used. She pulled it close to the bed and waited for Abigail to meet her eyes. "You need complete bed rest until it's time for your child to be born, Abigail. No cooking, no house cleaning, no laundry. You can walk to the bathroom and shower as needed, but other than that you are to stay in bed."

"Is that really…?" She swallowed past the anxiety clawing at her throat. "Is it necessary?"

"It is. We want you to carry this baby as near to term as possible. Your due date is mid-November, correct?"

Abigail nodded.

"Six weeks of bed rest, Abigail. That's our goal. Plus, weekly doctor's visits. Better yet, I'd like to sign you up to have a visiting nurse stop by your home. The less you're jostling around in a buggy, the better."

They spoke a few minutes longer. Abigail asked questions, and Dr. Rainey patiently answered them.

She recommended a hospital birth over a home birth.

She cautioned Abigail that if her condition worsened, if she experienced extreme headaches or sudden swelling, then she needed to return to the hospital immediately.

And when she learned that Abigail was a widow, she strongly advised that she not attempt to live alone. "You need someone with you at all times, Abigail...just in case."

Thomas understood that he could have left.

Luke assured him that they would take Abigail home when the doctor was ready to discharge her. Abigail hadn't asked him to stay. She probably didn't even realize he was still there. Duchess stood in the parking area, in the rain, wondering why her supper was late.

He could have gone home to his little apartment above the mercantile.

But Thomas knew that the life of a bishop wasn't easy. Luke had his own children at home to look after. He also had a farm to run and animals to care for.

More than that, Thomas needed to see Abigail again. He needed to see with his own eyes that she was okay.

"I'll stay," he said, not even attempting to explain his reasoning. "And I can take her home when they release her."

Luke smiled and nodded as if he'd expected that answer.

Naomi returned to the waiting area and caught them up on what the doctor had said.

"You're sure she's going to be all right?" Thomas had told himself over and over that she would be, but hearing the words was like a cold salve over a recent burn.

"Oh, yes. She's much better already, and I suspect she'd like to see you, Thomas. But first there's something we need to discuss." She proceeded to tell them about the doctor's insistence that Abigail not live alone.

"I wonder if her parents or a sibling could come," Luke said. "I realize it will be a hardship. If I remember correctly, they live in Colorado."

Thomas cleared his throat, stared at his hands and finally said, "Abigail hasn't said much about her family, but from the little she has shared I don't think her *mamm* will help."

That sat between them for a few minutes.

It was Naomi who offered a solution. "*Mammi* Troyer."

Luke stroked his beard, considering, and finally smiled. "I believe you're right, dear. *Mammi* Troyer... I should have thought of it."

"You can't think of everything, even if you are the bishop."

"Ah." He winked at Thomas. "She keeps me well grounded."

"*Mammi* Troyer from your church district? Old *Mammi* Troyer? The woman has to be eighty at least. I did some work for

her a year or so ago…" Thomas didn't like
the idea at all. There had to be someone
more dependable that they could think of,
someone younger and stronger who could
stay with Abigail until her *boppli* was
born. "How can she be of any help? And
are you sure she'll be willing to…move in
with Abigail?"

"I suspect she will." Luke stood, stuck
his hands in his pockets and jingled some
change there. "And you would be surprised
how spry *Mammi* is. It's true that she won't
be out feeding the horse…"

"*Nein*, I'll feed the horse."

"But she still cooks and sews, and she'll
be *gut* company for Abigail."

Naomi seemed to think the matter was
settled. "The main thing is that Abigail not
be left alone. We can give her one of your
emergency cell phones."

Luke nodded in agreement.

"Yes. I think that would be appropriate."
He paused and added, "But Abigail should
call her *mamm* first and ask if she'd like
to come. She should give her *mamm* the

opportunity to bless her, and if she says no...then we ask *Mammi* Troyer."

He pulled his cell phone from his pocket and handed it to Thomas. "I suspect you'd like to visit with Abigail. Would you give this to her and see that she calls her parents?"

Yikes.

Thomas wasn't sure he wanted to do that at all. He wanted to see Abigail, but he didn't want to end up in the middle of a family squabble. He also didn't want to see Abigail cry, and for some reason he was fairly certain that talking to her *mamm* would result in that very thing. Unfortunately, he couldn't think of a single reason to tell the bishop no. So instead of making an excuse, he pocketed the cell phone and followed Naomi's directions back to Abigail's room...feeling for all the world like one of the martyrs of old, about to face his end.

He knocked, waited for her to answer, then opened the door and peeked inside. At the sight of her, he almost backed out.

Abigail was sitting up in her bed, no *kapp* on her head, brown hair tumbling around her shoulders. It had a touch of auburn to it. Why had he never noticed that before? It reminded him of the colors of fall.

He shook his head, attempting to refocus. A box of Kleenex was on her lap, and she was blotting her eyes. Good grief. She was crying, and he hadn't even told her the bad news yet.

"Come in, Thomas. I was..." She hiccupped, fresh tears spilling down her cheeks. "I was wanting to thank you."

"Hmm. Tears don't really convey that message."

He took the seat beside her bed and suddenly he knew that he wouldn't have backed out, even if she'd been sobbing or chucking things at him. He needed to see Abigail. He had to see, with his own eyes, that she was *oll recht*.

"You do look better, even though you're crying."

"I'm getting pretty sick of it…of crying, I mean."

"Then why do you do it?"

She pulled in a deep breath, which caused her to hiccup again. "I don't know. I never was much of a crier before, but now it seems as if my eyes—and my heart— have a mind of their own."

He didn't know what to say to that, and he couldn't keep looking at her or he'd pull her back into his arms. The memory of the feel of her against him as he'd carried her to the buggy was still fresh. For one moment the restlessness in the center of his being had stopped and been replaced by…

By what?

Love? Did he honestly think he was in love? His eyes darted around the room, searching for something to land on other than the woman in the bed beside him. He wasn't in love with Abigail Yutzy. She was a widow and seven months pregnant to boot.

"You look as if you've seen a pig fly."

"A pig fly?"

"Something my *daddi* used to say. He was a funny old guy—so unlike my *dat*."

Thomas felt relief that they'd moved to solid ground and she'd stopped crying. He relaxed back into the chair. "This was your *dat*'s father, then?"

"Right. He lived with us for a time, not in a *dawdi haus* because my parents didn't have the funds to build one."

"But the community would…"

"Colorado's Amish community is quite small. There are less people, and the land is much harder to farm. Plus, my parents would have never let it be known that they needed a *dawdi haus*. But when *Daddi* came to live with us, he brightened up the place. My parents have always seemed quite stern to me, but *Daddi* was…different."

"You loved him."

"I love them all, but I enjoyed being around him." She plucked at the hospital blanket. "They say I can't stay alone, Thomas. I don't know what to do."

"Luke and Naomi had some ideas on

that. But first, tell me how you're feeling and what the doctor said." He'd heard most of the details from Naomi, but he wanted to hear them from Abigail. He also wanted to know if she'd understood the doctor's instructions in the same way that Naomi had.

It only took a few minutes for her to go over all the tests and the results. She only smiled once, when she told him that she was having a girl.

"*Ya?* That's *wunderbaar.*"

"It is. I would have loved a boy, of course, but I feel like I would have known less about how to raise one."

"I guess they're pretty much the same at that age."

"Maybe." She crossed her arms over her stomach and stared at the blanket. Her voice—when she finally spoke—was small and trembly. "What am I going to do, Thomas?"

"About living alone?"

"*Ya.* I don't know anyone that well. And the people I do know, they all have families to care for." She looked up at him now, as if she expected him to have an answer.

Which he did, but she wasn't going to like it.

"Luke and Naomi know someone who they think will be happy to come and stay with you."

"Really?"

"*Ya.*"

"Who?"

"*Mammi* Troyer."

Abigail shook her head. "I don't think I know who that is."

"I worked for her once. She's a nice lady."

"Ugh. Having a stranger stay with me every day..."

"It's not for the rest of your life, Abigail. Just until your *doschder* is born."

And that word—*doschder*—softened the stubborn look that had crept onto her face.

"You're right. Okay. I'll do it."

"There's one more thing." He pulled the cell phone from his pocket. "They want you to call your parents first."

Abigail's expression had turned to one

of puzzlement. "Why? Why would I do that?"

"How did Luke say it…?" He studied his hands, then glanced up at her. "He said you should give them the opportunity to bless you."

"Obviously he doesn't know my *mamm*."

Thomas thought that perhaps Abigail was being a bit dramatic, but then he could relate to where she might be coming from. He hadn't been raised by exemplary parents either. His *mamm* had done the best she could, which, looking back, he realized wasn't good at all. His *dat*'s behavior was owing to his addiction.

He understood bad parenting, but he also believed that at some point you picked yourself up and moved on with your life.

"Is she that bad?"

Abigail didn't answer. She held out her hand, and he dropped the old-style flip phone into her palm. An Amish bishop might occasionally carry a phone, in some progressive districts, but it wouldn't be what the *Englischers* called a smartphone.

Nothing smart about the small black device that Abigail was holding.

"Will you have to leave a message at the phone shack?"

"*Nein.* Most every Plain farmer in Monte Vista has a side business, and every side business has a phone in the office area. It's not attached to the house, of course. But chances are that someone will hear it ringing even though they've already closed up for the day." She glanced up at the clock, which showed it was nearly nine in the evening.

They would be out in the work area at nine in the evening? Most Amish people that Thomas knew were asleep by that time. Then he remembered the time change—it would be two hours earlier in Colorado.

"Do you want me to give you some privacy?"

"*Nein,* I'd rather you stay." Then she pulled in a deep breath and punched in her parents' number.

The conversation was rather short. Abigail gave the brief version of her current situation. Thomas couldn't hear how her *mamm* replied, but Abigail's portion of the conversation told him what he needed to know.

"*Ya.* Of course."

"I understand."

"*Ya, Mamm.*"

"All right. You've made yourself quite clear."

Between each statement, her *mamm* must have lectured some more. At one point, Abigail set the phone down on top of her stomach and stared up at the ceiling. Apparently, when she picked it up, her *mamm* was still talking. Finally, she said goodbye, pushed a button on the phone and handed it back to Thomas.

"That didn't sound *gut.*"

"About what I expected."

"Meaning…"

"Meaning that she had planned to come and see me after Thanksgiving, and that a little baby scare wasn't enough reason to change her plans."

"But you need someone to stay with you. I heard you tell her that…at the beginning."

Abigail shrugged. Finally, she said, "My *mamm*'s a big believer in learning to handle things on your own."

Thomas didn't understand, but apparently Abigail wasn't going to say anything else on the subject.

Instead, she squared her shoulders. "Looks like it's *Mammi* Troyer or no one."

Oh, there would be someone. If *Mammi* said no, and Thomas doubted that would happen, then a barrage of women would set up a schedule with four-hour shifts. Abigail would not be left alone to handle this.

As for Thomas, he was already wondering if he should move into the barn until the baby was born.

Chapter Seven

Abigail ended up spending the night at the hospital. It took longer than the doctor had hoped to bring her blood pressure down to a safe level. The next morning, she woke up early, having slept better than she had in a long time. After receiving the nurse's permission, she showered, put on the clothes she'd been wearing the day before and ate the breakfast they brought.

There was a knock on her door, and Clare King stuck her head in. "I heard there was an Amish woman in here...ready to break out."

"I am! But what are you doing here?"

"The kids are with Saul's *mamm*. She

lives next door." She walked into the room and sank onto a chair. "So. Have you been watching soap operas?"

Abigail laughed. "I haven't even turned the television on."

"I guess you've been pretty tired." Clare reached across and grasped her hand. "Everyone has been praying. You're feeling better?"

"Yes, but how did you even know I was here?"

Clare shrugged her shoulders. "You know how it is. Amish grapevine."

They both smiled at that.

"Also, I'm here to give you a ride home."

Which was exactly what Abigail needed to hear. Within an hour, she was discharged. They went by the pharmacy to pick up her prescription, and then Clare turned her buggy toward Abigail's house.

"It'll be nice to be home."

"You were gone less than a day."

They both laughed. The sun was shining, and the air was crisp. It was hard to believe that it was October, and by mid-November, she'd be a *mamm*. She supposed that technically she already was, but by the time Thanksgiving came around, she'd be holding her baby girl in her arms.

Abigail told Clare that the doctor didn't want her to stay alone and that Naomi thought *Mammi* Troyer would come.

Clare nodded in approval. "You know *Mammi*, don't you?"

"I don't think so."

"She sits with the older women."

"I feel terrible, but I don't really know many people's names."

Clare glanced at her, then refocused on the road. "*Mammi* is special. We all think so."

They pulled into Abigail's drive. Thomas waved them toward the front porch.

"Say, how do you like having Thomas work for you?"

"I like it, I guess. I wish I didn't need the help, but since I do…"

"He's handsome. Don't you think?"

Abigail felt her cheeks warm. She'd been

thinking that very thing. One glance at Clare, and they both fell to laughing again.

"I act like a *youngie* when I'm around you," she confessed.

"Is that so bad?"

"I suppose not."

Clare called out to her horse, pulled on the reins and then set the brake on the buggy.

Thirty minutes later, Abigail had changed clothes and was in bed. "This feels ridiculous," she muttered. "It's the middle of the day."

"I've put your baby books on the side table, along with a glass of water." Clare bent down and gave her a hug. "Oh, and Thomas wants you to have this."

She handed her a whistle. "I threaded a piece of the baby ribbon you had left over through it. That way, you can wear it around your neck."

"I'm supposed to wear it?"

"He says that he'll be able to hear that whistle anywhere on the property."

"You don't say."

"Give it a try. Let's see how long it takes him to get here." Her eyes were sparkling, and she wiggled her eyebrows, daring Abigail to blow on the whistle.

Abigail shook her head, laughter bubbling up inside of her. Oh, Clare did help her to see the fun in things.

She gave the whistle a solid blow, causing them both to clap their hands over their ears. Clare watched the second hand on the clock and at the twenty-five-second mark, Thomas burst through the door.

"What is it? What's wrong? Do you need to go back to the hospital?"

Abigail felt a twinge of guilt for causing him to worry. "*Nein, nein.* I was just... practicing."

Then Thomas noticed Clare trying to hide her laughter behind her hands.

"Oh, very funny. Were you timing me?"

"Say, Thomas. I have to go." Clare picked up her purse and pulled on her coat, catching Abigail's gaze and nearly sending her into another fit of laughter. "You'll be here with Abigail until *Mammi* comes, right?"

"*Ya.* Sure."

"We don't even know for certain that she's coming," Abigail protested.

Clare and Thomas shared a look that Abigail couldn't quite interpret.

"What's going on?"

Thomas shrugged, then admitted, "Actually, Luke stopped by earlier. I told him Clare would help you get settled, and he said to tell you *Mammi* would be here midafternoon."

Abigail rolled her eyes heavenward.

This being taken care of was amusing at first, but she wasn't sure she had the patience for it. Then she thought of her *doschder,* remembered the doctor's look of concern and nodded.

She'd find the patience, somehow.

Because being inconvenienced was nothing when compared to the safety of her *boppli.*

Clare told her to get some rest.

Thomas reminded her he'd be just outside.

Once she was alone in her room, Abigail

had every intention of reading through one of the baby books someone had left for her, but she ended up sleeping through most of the afternoon. She woke to the sound of voices outside—Thomas and a woman. It must be *Mammi* Troyer. Abigail glanced at the clock. It was nearly four in the afternoon. Maybe she was coming by to say hello, and to let her know she'd spend the next day with her. Abigail almost hopped up to greet her at the door, but she remembered she was supposed to stay in bed.

She was stewing over that when *Mammi* and Thomas appeared at her bedroom door. Thomas stood behind her, towered over her really. Perhaps it was the contrast between the two that caused *Mammi* to seem so small. The woman must have been just shy of five feet and couldn't have weighed a hundred pounds. Her face was a virtual map of wrinkles and her white hair peeked from her *kapp*. She wore large owlish glasses that magnified her blue eyes, and she walked with a cane.

Oh boy.

Who was going to be helping whom?

But that wasn't the worst of it. When *Mammi* stepped into the room, Abigail was able to see that Thomas was carrying a suitcase. A suitcase? Why did *Mammi* bring a suitcase?

Mammi might be small, old and need a cane, but she moved with amazing agility. She was beside Abigail's bed in a flash, straightening the covers and tsking.

"You must be Abigail. I've heard so much about you, child."

"And you're *Mammi* Troyer."

"Just *Mammi* is fine. It's what everyone calls me. One of the advantages of being old is that you become everyone's grand-mother." *Mammi* sat in the chair beside Abigail's bed, but turned her attention to Thomas.

"You can leave the suitcase in the sitting room, Thomas. I'll make myself quite comfortable on the couch."

She was going to sleep on the couch?

"As for the other boxes, just stack them

in the kitchen. We'll get to them as we need them."

Abigail looked up at Thomas, a dozen questions lingering on her lips. He mouthed, "Be nice," then ducked out of the room. What did that mean? When was she not nice?

She turned back to *Mammi* and plastered on a smile. "I didn't realize you would be staying overnight."

"More than overnight. I'll be here until your *boppli* arrives." And then she leaned forward and put her hands on Abigail's stomach, nearly causing Abigail to jump out of the covers.

If *Mammi* noticed her startled reaction, she didn't comment on it. In fact, her eyes were closed and she began to pray aloud— for Abigail's child, for Abigail's doctor, for Thomas and Luke and Naomi and herself. And then she prayed that *Gotte* would keep his hand upon Abigail, that He would care for her as He cared for the sparrow, and would protect and guide her.

Abigail thought the tears would start to flow again.

Other than Thomas carrying her outside, no one had touched her for so long. Oh, there was the occasional hand clasp from Clare, the pat on her arm from Naomi. This was different. *Mammi*'s hands on her stomach felt like a blessing. For the first time in a very long time, Abigail was able to breathe deeply. The anxiety that seemed to always reside in her belly fled.

Possibly for the first time since moving to Shipshewana, Abigail had the hope that maybe everything was going to be all right.

Thomas had no reason to go back into the house before he left for the day, but neither did he feel good just driving away. Best to be sure. He climbed the porch steps, knocked the dirt and mud off his shoes and tapped lightly on the door. Thinking both of the women might be in the back of the house, he opened the front door and stuck his head inside.

What he saw then surprised him.

Abigail was lying on her left side on the couch, a pillow behind her head and a knitted blanket covering her. She glanced up from the book she was reading. With a smile, she motioned him into the room, then turned the book so that he could see a picture of various vegetables and fruits.

"My *doschder* is the size of a coconut, or maybe a honeydew melon."

"Ya?" He took the book and pretended to study it. His eyes fell to the image beside week thirty-nine, and he almost dropped the book. Her stomach was going to be as big as a watermelon? Literally? He snapped the book shut and set it on the coffee table.

"I see you've moved to the living room."

"Yup. *Mammi* said that it wasn't *gut* to stay in one room all day. She's dealt with preeclampsia before. She said that lying on the couch was every bit as *gut* as lying on the bed."

"Did she now?"

"It definitely helps my mood to be out of my bedroom for a few hours."

He didn't point out that she'd only been home a few hours or that she had six weeks to go. Probably best not to bring either up right now. "Everything's *gut*?"

"*Ya.*" Abigail lowered her voice. "I didn't realize *Mammi* was going to live here."

"Ah."

"Doesn't she have…family?"

"Not anymore. She had a husband and two sons, but she outlived them both."

"She must have *grandkinner.*"

"Oh, sure. The daughters-in-law remarried over twenty years ago. They all live in Goshen now. She sees them several times a year."

"Why doesn't she live with them?"

Thomas shrugged. "Stubborn, maybe? I did some work on her place a while ago. She leased out the fields, but she needed help putting in her vegetable garden."

"I can't imagine her sleeping on the couch." Abigail worried her thumbnail before blurting out, "She's eighty if she's a day. I think I should give her my room…"

"You'll do no such thing," *Mammi* called out from the kitchen.

Abigail pressed her fingers to her lips, though whether it was because *Mammi* had overheard her or to stop from laughing, Thomas wasn't sure.

He leaned forward and said in a very loud whisper, "Her hearing is freakishly good for someone her age."

"Indeed, it is," *Mammi* called out.

Thomas and Abigail shared a smile.

Finally, Thomas said, "Let me think on the bed problem. I might know someone who has an extra bed I could bring over."

"She's only here for six weeks, though."

"Six weeks on a couch can seem like a long time."

Mammi appeared at the archway that separated the kitchen from the sitting room. "Your generation has been blessed more than you realized. These old bones have spent many a night sleeping in a hayloft, or on a porch, or even on the floor. A few weeks on a couch won't hurt me a bit."

She turned back toward the kitchen, then

pivoted toward them. "Soup's nearly ready. Will you stay with us, Thomas?"

He looked to Abigail, who nodded enthusiastically.

"I'd love to. *Danki.*"

The meal did more to ease Thomas's worries than a thousand assurances would have. Abigail was relaxed around *Mammi,* as if she could finally stop showing such a tough exterior to the entire world. Who wouldn't be a *gut* patient under *Mammi's* supervision? The woman was strangely convincing for someone so small in stature.

The soup was delicious, served with fresh bread and thick slices of cheese. Abigail would be eating better as long as *Mammi* was there.

But more than the food or the sleeping arrangement, *Mammi* had managed to bring a warmth to the little house that hadn't been there before. Perhaps having someone close by would do more than provide Abigail a measure of safety; perhaps

Mammi's presence would begin to heal her heart.

He drew the line when *Mammi* stood up to do the dishes.

"*Nein.* You fed me. It's only fair that I clean up."

"A man doing the dishes?" Abigail rubbed her stomach and tried to look shocked. "I might faint."

Mammi laughed along with Abigail. "My Joshua always did the dishes with me. Unless I was pregnant, then he insisted I sit on the porch or in the living room and let him tidy up. He was a *gut* man."

"How long has he been gone?" Abigail's tone had turned suddenly serious.

"Fourteen years, and I still miss him. That never changes when you lose someone you love, but the pain? Well, the pain left after a time, and for that I thank the good Lord."

Thomas drove home that night less worried than he had been since first climbing the steps to Abigail's house.

There were still a lot of questions, and

those piled up on him as he drove back to his small apartment. How would Abigail manage for the next six weeks? How would she care for the baby alone once it was born? What would become of Asher's estate? And what was with her own mother? How could the woman have refused to come to Shipshe and care for Abigail?

His shoulders slumped under the questions until, by the time he climbed the steps to his apartment, he felt as if he were eighty years old.

It was a job, nothing more.

He shouldn't take Abigail's problems so personally.

Only they felt personal, and he kept remembering holding her in his arms.

Though he had eaten at Abigail's, he was still hungry. He'd turned down second helpings, thinking she and *Mammi* might be able to eat it for lunch the next day. Now his stomach growled, reminding him that he'd put in a full day of work. Instead of making a sandwich, he dumped cereal into a bowl, poured milk over it and stood at the kitchen counter eating.

He was getting too close; that was the problem. Abigail had handled things before he'd arrived. He remembered the goat blocking her front porch steps and shook his head. Mostly, she had handled things— other than the goat and the harvest and the vegetable garden.

The barn's roof needed patching, and there were sections of fence that needed to be shored up before the snow started piling against it.

He finished his dinner, set the bowl in the sink and filled it with water.

The truth was that Abigail needed him, whether she realized it or not. She didn't need him in the house, though. She had *Mammi* now. Problem solved. He'd stay away from the house—stay in the barn and the fields.

As he readied for bed, he vowed that he would not look at any more baby books.

Though the image of a watermelon-sized stomach was enough to give him nightmares. He climbed into his own bed and doused the light.

If you had a stomach that large, how would you turn over in bed at night? How would you stand up? How would you carry it around all day long?

He'd never thought of those things when his *schweschdern* were pregnant. Somehow, he'd imagined the process involved a few months of being larger and then you have a *boppli*. Easy enough.

He tossed onto his other side.

Abigail would be fine. He didn't need to worry about her. He needed to do his job and not get involved.

That was the ticket.

Don't get involved.

But a voice followed him into his dreams, taunting him, and telling him that it was a bit late for that.

Chapter Eight

The first week that *Mammi* stayed with Abigail, everything went smoothly enough.

Yes, Abigail was tired of lying around.

Yes, she was ready to have this *boppli* and move on to being a *mamm*.

And also yes, she understood the importance of giving her *doschder* as much time in the womb as possible. That last reason was more than enough. She let *Mammi* do the cooking. Clare and Naomi stopped by twice a week to help with the laundry and cleaning. Abigail was allowed to bathe, occasionally sit up on the couch, read and knit.

Turned out that one of *Mammi*'s boxes

had been full of books—pregnancy books, devotional books, baby's-first-year books, gardening books, quilting books and even knitting books.

Another box had been filled with fabric, thread, quilt batting, yarn and knitting needles.

When Abigail had confessed that she didn't know how to quilt or knit, *Mammi* had smiled and clapped her hands. "*Wunderbaar*, I will teach you."

Every day they spent at least two hours in the morning and two in the afternoon working on their projects. It was oddly satisfying to create something with her own hands, though her knitting projects tended to have skipped stitches, and her quilting was uneven at best.

"No single thing on this Earth is perfect, Abigail. I've had *Englischers* ask if we put a mistake in every quilt." *Mammi* hooted—the laughter, combined with the large glasses, caused her to resemble an owl more than ever. "As if we'd need to put a mistake in something. There are always mistakes. But we press on, doing the very best that we can."

Mammi would sometimes tell Abigail about her family. She'd describe their first home and what Shipshewana had been like then, before tourists had discovered the area. She would talk about her sons, both of whom had died in their fifties—one from cancer and the other from a heart attack, just two years apart. She sometimes quoted Scriptures about the heavenly reunion they had to look forward to.

Every day when they'd first pull out their projects, she'd throw out a proverb, as if it could focus their efforts.

Pride in your work puts joy in your day.

Burying your talents is a grave mistake.

Pray for a good harvest but continue to hoe.

Some of these sayings made sense to Abigail—others didn't. A few even seemed related to what they were doing. Regardless, she found that she enjoyed their time working together. It was a real joy to sit with someone else, whether they talked or not. Perhaps that's why she so quickly accepted *Mammi* as a part of her family, as a part of her life.

As promised, Thomas had found a bed for her and set it up in the baby's room. Since it was a twin, it fit easily. And since *Mammi* was so small, a twin-size bed was plenty big enough.

Yes, her life was better with *Mammi* in it. Abigail could almost be grateful for the emergency scare that had landed her on bed rest. Almost.

While her relationship with *Mammi* grew richer and more important to her each day, the same couldn't be said of her relationship with Thomas. It seemed that Thomas, mysteriously, was suddenly too busy for coffee in the morning, oatmeal bars in the afternoon or stew in the evening.

Once, she actually caught him looking longingly toward the kitchen. He was standing as close to the front door as possible, his back practically pressed against it. He'd stepped inside to update her on what he'd done on the farm that day.

"Why don't you stay for dinner? You know you want to, and *Mammi* has made plenty of food."

She thought he might cave, but the wall that had sprung up between them held firm. "Can't. Gotta go...do some paperwork." And he was out of there as if Abigail were pursuing him with a dirty diaper and a wet mop.

Only there were no dirty diapers yet.

And no one would let her anywhere near a mop.

What was the man so afraid of? He was acting as if Abigail had a contagious disease. He was acting as if the night when he'd carried her to the buggy had never happened.

She sighed as she gazed out the front window and watched his horse trot away.

Finally, she picked up her knitting. She'd found that when she was agitated, the simple rhythm of knitting helped to calm her thoughts and feelings.

Unfortunately, she kept thinking of Thomas looking anywhere but at her. Thomas fiddling with his hat as if he didn't know what to do with his hands. Thomas practically sprinting from her house.

Mammi brought her a hot cup of tea and set it on the coffee table.

"Danki."

Mammi cocked her head, then sat in the chair opposite the couch. "Problem, dear?"

"With the knitting? *Nein*." Abigail stared down at her nice, even stitches. She was making a crib blanket of the softest pink-and-lavender yarn—another gift from *Mammi*'s knitting box.

"Thank you for teaching me to make a blanket."

"Next week we'll start on a wee sweater. You're a fast learner, Abigail."

Why did the tiniest compliment cause her spirits to lift so? Maybe because she wasn't used to it. Asher had never been one to throw around praise, which she had thought was normal since her *mamm* didn't either.

Her *mamm*.

The memory of their phone conversation still caused her anger to flare. Or was it shame? Was she ashamed of calling her *mamm* and asking for help? Or was she ashamed of her *mamm*'s quick response— a resounding no?

She cleared her throat and focused again on the yarn and needles in her hands. "My *mamm* wasn't much of a craftsy person. She always said it was cheaper to buy what we needed at yard sales."

"Undoubtedly, your *mamm* was right about that." Abigail removed her large glasses and wiped her eyes. Then she cast about looking for the glasses.

"They're beside you—on the table."

"Ah. *Danki.*"

"*Gem gschehne.*"

Mammi was always losing her glasses,

and they were usually within arm's reach. It was absolutely adorable.

"So why do we do it? Why do we knit if my *mamm* was right?"

"Knitting, crocheting, cooking, even cleaning...the things we do are works of love. The question isn't always what is easiest or what is least expensive—sometimes we simply need to do something that shows another person how much we care."

Abigail thought of Thomas describing the patches he'd put on the barn's roof. She'd thought he was so proud of himself, but perhaps he was trying to tell her he cared.

Ridiculous.

The man had words. He knew how to speak. If he cared, he could say so. She pushed away thoughts of Thomas, something she had to do with an increasing frequency these days.

"I like knitting for my *boppli*. It makes me feel...connected to her."

"Indeed, and it's a *gut* use of your time. No doubt your baby girl will pass these things on to her baby girl. It'll be a lineage of love."

A lineage of love.

Tears sprang to Abigail's eyes at the thought, and she blinked rapidly.

"I didn't mean to upset you," *Mammi* said softly.

Mammi was old, but she noticed everything. She was maybe the most perceptive person that Abigail had ever known.

"I was thinking of my *mamm* and wondering why there was no lineage of love there."

"Perhaps you're being a bit hard on her."

"She isn't here, is she? *Nein.* She couldn't come to care for her own *doschder.* She couldn't change her plans." Abigail tugged roughly on the yarn. "Her exact words. 'Abigail, I've already made my plans to come after the baby is born. I'm sure you'll be fine. You need to learn to stand on your own two feet.'"

"Hard to stand on your own two feet when the doctor insists on bed rest." *Mammi*'s eyes twinkled, but there was also compassion in the woman's gaze. "Tell me about your relationship with your *mamm*."

"Not much to tell. She had seven children. I have three older *bruders* and three younger *schweschdern*. My parents live in Monte Vista, Colorado, but my siblings all scattered as quickly as they could." Abigail's hands fell still in her lap. Why did the memories of home hurt so much? She shook her head. "What I mean is, they moved away—all but the youngest two. It's expected of us in some unsaid way. When I turned twenty-four and was still home, my *mamm* decided she needed to speak to the bishop about an arranged marriage. Our bishop spoke with Bishop Luke here, who knew Asher. And the rest is…well, it isn't Cinderella, but it's my story."

"I think Cinderella is overrated."

"What do you mean?"

Unlike Abigail, when *Mammi* spoke, her knitting didn't slow at all. Her needles were a virtual blur. And what was she making with that yellow-and-pink yarn? It reminded Abigail of spring.

"I mean none of us need talking mice or a pumpkin that turns into a carriage. We only need to have faith and believe."

"That's what landed me here. I had faith that my *mamm* and bishop knew best. I believed that it would all work out and I'd somehow have a better life."

Mammi stopped knitting, cocked her head and looked at her. "Do you regret that? Marrying Asher, moving here, getting pregnant? If you had known it would end up this way, would you have stayed in Colorado?"

Abigail didn't have to think about that answer for very long. "*Nein*. I'm happier here—alone, or rather with you and Luke and Naomi and Clare..."

"And Thomas."

Abigail shrugged. "I'm happier here, even in my precarious situation, than I ever was at home."

They knitted another few minutes, and Abigail thought the subject had been dropped when *Mammi* suddenly stood, then moved around the coffee table and sat beside her on the couch. Abigail was sitting with her feet propped on the coffee table atop a pillow.

Mammi covered Abigail's hands with her own. "There's something I want to say to you about your *mamm*."

Now Abigail fervently wished she hadn't brought up the subject. Talking about it never helped. People invariably supported her *mamm*, pointing out that having seven children wasn't easy and that living in Colorado in a small Plain community was no doubt hard. She hadn't really talked to anyone but her siblings about it, and she'd given up on that long ago.

The past is the past, Abigail. Move on.

Why couldn't she move on?

Mammi was still waiting for a response, so Abigail nodded.

"I want you to remember that someone cannot show what they haven't learned." She smiled and waited.

"That's it?"

"*Ya.*"

"I don't understand."

Mammi nodded as if she'd expected that response. "What was your mother's mother like?"

"I don't remember."

"Hmm. Well, I'm just guessing here, but often when people don't know how to show affection, it's because they never had affection shown to them."

"Sounds like an excuse to me."

"Is it? Could you have knitted if I hadn't shown you how?"

"Probably not. I've tried before, and it always just turned into a knot of yarn."

"Exactly. We can sometimes learn from reading about a thing, or from watching others, but mainly we learn from experience. Based on what you have shared with me, your *mamm* was raised to provide a clean home, *gut* meals and yard sale clothing. If she didn't cuddle you as a child, perhaps she herself wasn't cuddled as a child. How would she know that you needed cuddling?"

"I thought that was intuitive."

"Perhaps. But our history often drowns out our intuition."

"I guess."

Mammi reached out for Abigail's shoulders and pulled her into an awkward hug—but it was only awkward because they were sitting sideways on the couch. Otherwise, it was becoming quite familiar, quite comfortable, to have *Mammi* give her a hug or kiss her cheek or even reach out and squeeze her hands.

Abigail swiped at her tears. "Your *mamm* must have been a *gut* mother."

"Oh, she was that." And then *Mammi* said the words that Abigail had sorely needed to hear. "And you will be a *gut mamm* too, Abigail. You will give your *boppli* all the cuddling and hugging that she needs. And you'll also provide for her in practical ways, because you learned that from your *mamm.*"

"I hope so."

"You can be sure. Blessed Assurance, *ya*?"

"*Ya.*" She was suddenly too tired to knit

another stitch. *Mammi* toddled off to check on the soup she was making, and Abigail stretched out on the couch, pulled the blanket atop herself and tried to imagine being a mother—being a good mother.

She might be able to do that.

She was learning so much from *Mammi*.

But the one thing she couldn't do was be a good mother *and* father. It broke her heart to think her *doschder* would be raised without a father, but really what could she do about that? It wasn't as if she could advertise for a husband. Bishop Luke might know of someone who was looking to marry, but an arranged relationship hadn't worked out so well the last time she'd tried it. She didn't want someone who was merely lonely or someone who felt pity for her.

What she wanted was the kind of love that *Mammi* had shared with her husband, Joshua. Images of Thomas popped into her mind. Thomas shooing the goat off her front porch. Thomas telling her to stop crying. Thomas carrying her to the buggy.

She thought of those moments much too often.

Thomas had never misled her. For reasons she couldn't fathom, he was not interested in marrying. At least he'd never broached the subject with her. *Nein*, she'd be better off not daydreaming about such things.

As she closed her eyes, she placed her hand on her stomach and tried to convey her love to her *doschder*. They would make it on their own. They'd have to.

The next few weeks were difficult ones for Thomas. He was a man being torn in opposite directions. On the one hand, he needed to see Abigail every day, to see for himself that she was fine, and to calm the anxiousness building in his heart. On the other hand, he understood what was happening.

He had a crush on Abigail Yutzy.

It had to be a crush. There was no chance it was something more serious. She was a widow. She was in the last trimester of her pregnancy, and she was his employer. It couldn't be love. Love happened when two people courted, when they realized they were right for each other, when they had shared experiences that brought them closer together. Okay, they had shared a few experiences, but that alone wasn't enough to build a relationship on. There wasn't even a small chance that what he was feeling could be more serious than a crush.

Those thoughts muddled his mind as he sat in the office of the mercantile, supposedly helping Mary Lehman.

"What you're feeling isn't so strange, if you think about it." Mary nodded as if she saw this sort of thing all the time, and perhaps she did—with seven children, three already married, it wasn't as if matters of the heart were a new topic for her.

She had yet to meet Abigail.

Perhaps that made it easier for Thomas to talk to her. Plus, he'd always viewed Mary as a surrogate mother, probably because she'd willingly embraced the role.

"Think about it, Thomas. You like to rescue things. That could actually be a tag line for your business. We Rescue the Lost." She held her hand up and waved it left to right, as if she could see the words painted in giant letters on the side of his buggy. "Of course, there's no *we* in your business, but it sounds better if you're not a one-man show. Gives you more respectability."

Thomas was putting sticky labels on handmade Christmas cards: $4.99 Each. Amish Made.

He could see something being worth more because it was handmade. That made it original, but the fact that it was Amish made…how did that make it worth $4.99 instead of $3.99?

"It's not even Thanksgiving yet," he muttered. "Why am I tagging Christmas cards?"

"Because you need something to do with your hands. Tell me why you're home early."

Actually, it wasn't that early. The clock

on the wall read ten minutes past six, and the store was already closed. He'd found Mary in the small office, finishing up a few tasks because her *doschder* was making dinner that night.

"You were home by four. You're rarely home before dark."

"Oh, *ya*. I guess I was done at Abigail's, and there was no logical reason to hang around."

"I'm glad you came down to see me."

Her smile assured him that this was the truth. He never felt like he was putting Mary out or that he was in the way. She was a *gut* person—a *gut* friend.

"Besides, it's better you're down here doing something useful, than upstairs pacing back and forth. I thought you were going to wear a path in the floor."

He put a label on upside down, then tried to cover it up with another. In the process, he managed to stick two more labels to his fingers. Finally, he dropped it all on her desk. "Here. I'm just messing this up."

"Hmm. Perhaps a mug of hot tea is what you need."

He started to argue. He did not need hot tea, and he was sure she should be headed home. But he didn't say any of that. He sat there and let her heat water in the electric kettle she kept in the office—they had electricity in the store. Thomas had it in his home, though he didn't use it. What would he use it on? It wasn't like he had a television or computer or stereo system.

She pushed a mug of herbal tea into his hands.

"Talk to me." Her voice was quiet, low, patient.

Perhaps her gentle attitude was why he was able to voice his confusion. Mary Lehman didn't push, but she had the patience of Job. Best to confess all so that she could go home to her family.

"It's like I care about her, but maybe more than I should. Or in a different way than I should. And I know it's ridiculous, so I vow that I'm going to put the entire thing out of my mind. That only succeeds in me thinking about her even more." He sipped the tea, closing his eyes and inhaling the aroma. When he opened his eyes again, Mary was still waiting. "I don't know what to do about it. I could quit the job, but that would leave her in a bind. Who else is going to work for deferred wages? But I'm worried that if I stay, this...infatuation...will only grow worse."

When she still didn't respond, he added a bit gruffly, "Maybe there's some herb or natural remedy you could give me."

"Oh, Thomas. There's no remedy for love."

"Love? Who said I was in love?"

"You did. You just don't realize it yet." She set aside her own mug of tea, crossed her arms on the desk and leaned forward. "I could argue with nearly everything you said."

"But..."

"How can you care about someone more than you should?"

"That's the thing..."

"Why is it ridiculous for you to care about Abigail?"

"Because she's married."

"Was married."

"She's pregnant."

"That will resolve itself in a few weeks."

Thomas pushed away the mug of tea and buried his head in his hands, tugging fistfuls of his hair in the hopes of calming his spinning thoughts.

"And quitting...when have you ever quit on someone?"

He opened his mouth, then shut it because they both knew the answer to that—never.

Mary stood and walked to his side of the desk. Sitting in the chair next to him, she waited until he raised his eyes to hers. "John and I think of you as our son. You've shared with us on numerous occasions your worries that you would be like your *dat*, your fear of trusting your emotions. But, Thomas... *Gotte* is doing a new thing in you. And you know what? You can trust Him."

"I don't know how to do that." His voice was a whisper.

"Sometimes it's as simple as taking the next step. Stop fighting what you're feeling and start praying."

"Praying?"

"Ask *Gotte* what He wants you to do next."

He stared past her now, at the far wall of the office that held a calendar. The page was turned to November. He'd known Abigail nearly two months. How could his life turn upside down in such a short time?

"Can I give you some advice?"

"I thought you just did."

"No one receives unlimited chances. No one has an endless string of days in front of them. It's the worst kind of arrogance to believe that you do." Then she kissed him on top of the head—making him feel like a child but also bringing an odd sense of comfort to his troubled soul—and walked out of the room.

Four hours later, the store's phone rang. The incessant ringing woke him from a dream of springtime fields that he couldn't seem to plant. Every time he'd reach the end of the row and turn the horses, he'd find that he hadn't started yet. He sat up in bed, realized it was the phone that he was hearing, and barreled downstairs.

There was only one person who would be calling the store at this hour.

"Abigail's in labor." *Mammi*'s voice sounded as calm as if she were giving him the weather report.

Thomas sent up a silent prayer of thanksgiving that Luke had left the cell phone with her.

"Can you come and fetch us, take us to the hospital?"

"Me?"

"*Ya*. We called Luke, but he was staying at a member's house, sitting with their *daddi* so the family could go out of town for the birth of a *grandkinner*."

"Okay. *Ya*. Of course. I'm on my way." He hung up the phone and rushed upstairs. Grabbing his hat and coat, he sprinted back down the stairs. It wasn't until he opened the outer door that he realized he'd forgotten about getting properly dressed.

He dashed back upstairs, threw on a shirt, pants and suspenders, then his shoes—not bothering with socks. He'd broken into a sweat by the time he opened the barn door. How long did he have? Was Abigail having the baby right now? Would he arrive there to find he was too late? And what if everyone wasn't all right?

He pushed that thought away.

Pray.

Mary had told him to pray. So, he did. As he harnessed Duchess, he prayed for *Mammi* that she'd know what to do. He prayed for the doctors and nurses at the hospital, that they'd take good care of Abigail. He prayed for his horse and the roads and the weather and Bishop Luke. And then, as Duchess set off at a fast trot, he prayed for Abigail and her baby. That *Gotte* would care for them, protect them and hold them in the palm of His hand.

Chapter Nine

Mammi focused on guiding Abigail through deep breathing exercises. Abigail wasn't as frightened as she thought she might be. She was ready to meet her *doschder*. But the pain—the pain was a surprise. She'd known it would hurt, but she had never experienced anything like this before.

The contractions left her breathless. Her heart raced and sweat dripped down the back of her neck.

She was thinking of that, of sweating in the middle of a November evening, when the sound of a horse and buggy reached them.

"Sounds like our ride is here." *Mammi* hurried to open the door.

But it wasn't Bishop Luke who walked through the door. It was Thomas. Abigail remembered *Mammi* stepping out of the room to make the phone call, but she'd assumed the bishop would be the one to fetch her.

Thomas stood there, staring at her while he turned his hat round and round in his hands. He looked terrified. His face had lost all color—bleached whiter than their pine wood table. "It's time?"

"*Ya*. How'd you get here so fast?"

"Duchess is a *gut* horse." Thomas blinked rapidly, then stepped forward before backing up again. "Tell me what to do."

"We need to go to the hospital," *Mammi* explained. She'd donned her coat, a scarf and her bonnet. She'd picked up her knitting bag and purse and nodded at Abigail's small suitcase. "Let's get hopping. It's time for Abigail's *boppli* to greet the world."

"You're sure it's not..." His eyes met hers. "Like before?"

She shook her head, then realized another contraction was beginning. She squeezed her eyes shut and concentrated on breathing in small, rapid puffs. She clutched the arm of the couch so tightly that she expected to leave a palm print there. She lost herself in that little bubble that was the pain and her child and her body and the amazing thing that was called the miracle of birth.

"What's happening?" Thomas's voice was low, awed almost.

"She's breathing to help with the pain."

Thomas plopped into the chair. By the time Abigail opened her eyes, he was sitting there bent forward with his head between his knees.

"What's wrong with him?" Abigail managed to ask as she tried to pull in a steadying breath. They'd been timing the contractions. Currently, they were five minutes apart, which *Mammi* had declared was the perfect time to head to the hospital.

"Thomas." *Mammi* stood in front of Thomas and waited for him to look up.

When he did, she leaned forward and peered into his face. "Can you take us to the hospital?"

"Sure, *ya*. But shouldn't we call an ambulance?"

Abigail reached for the glass of water and downed half of it. When Thomas finally met her gaze, she couldn't read his expression. He was worried, of course. He'd never had a *boppli* and this entire situation must be making him uncomfortable. But there was something else in his gaze—something she couldn't quite understand.

"Buggy, please."

"Okay. Buggy. Got it." He stood and headed toward the back door, then remembered that he'd parked in the front. Pivoting he headed back through the living room and out the door. He popped back inside and picked up her suitcase, then paused to watch Abigail when she let out a little gasp and began breathing in puffs again.

She closed her eyes to better focus, but

she could still hear Thomas and *Mammi* talking.

"Is she going to be okay?"

"Oh, *ya*. For sure and certain, but this *boppli* is coming, Thomas. Let's shake a leg."

Abigail glanced up as *Mammi* pushed her knitting bag into his hands. "Take this to the buggy. Then come back and help Abigail."

She closed her eyes—focusing, breathing, praying. She heard the front door open and close, then open again. She looked up to see Thomas standing there next to her. He acted as if he was going to pick her up, like he had before, but she only shook her head and pushed herself into a standing position. She leaned on his arm, entwining her fingers with his, and his expression changed.

Looking down at her fingers clinging to his, Thomas's expression turned tender. When he looked up, the cocky grin that was so familiar to her was back. "You've got this, Abigail. Already, you're being a *gut mamm*."

"*Ya*. How do you figure?"

"Well, lots of women holler when they're in labor. You're not hollering."

"The night is young." She offered him a small smile, which seemed to be what he needed. Funny that she felt the need to comfort him when she was the one in labor. But she had read the books. She'd spoken with *Mammi* and Naomi and Clare. She knew what to expect, though she was finding that understanding a thing and experiencing it were quite different.

She was able to walk to the buggy, where Thomas scooped her up and set her in the back, next to *Mammi*. Another contraction was beginning, so Abigail didn't object to his helping her that way. Thomas called out to Duchess. Abigail closed her eyes and focused on her breathing.

Mammi counted in her soft voice, and when the contraction had passed, she said, "*Gut*. They're only four minutes apart now. This girl is impatient to meet her *mamm*."

The next hour was a blur.

She would lose herself in the bubble, in the pain and the miracle, and then events happening around her would come into focus.

The comforting sound of *Mammi*'s soft, calm voice.

Hurrying through the cold November night—Thomas urging Duchess into a steady trot.

Thomas helping Abigail into a wheelchair, and the look on his face when she thanked him.

Mammi and Thomas disappearing as the nurses pushed her wheelchair through the double doors.

Her last image of the two people who meant so much to her was of them sitting in the waiting room, huddled next to one another, *Mammi*'s hand on Thomas's back, both of them with their heads bowed in prayer.

Then the next contraction hit. This one brought with it an all-consuming pain that blocked out every other thought. She could hear the nurses calling for a doctor, and the familiar face of Dr. Rainey appeared above her saying, "Looks like you just made it, Abigail."

After that there was pushing and more pain and finally the cry of her *doschder* greeting the world.

Dr. Rainey placed the baby in her arms, and Abigail felt a rush of love unlike anything she'd ever experienced before. She gazed down into her *doschder*'s tiny, perfect face, then checked to make sure she had all her fingers and toes.

She was perfect.

"Do you have a name?" the doctor asked kindly.

"Joanna." She swiped at the tears on her cheeks. The name was right. She'd known it the moment she'd laid eyes on her baby. All those hours she'd spent paging through the *Big Book of Baby Names*. Now the moment was here, and she no longer wondered what she should name her baby girl. She just knew.

"That's a fine name, dear." Even the nurse

was beaming, but then who wouldn't smile looking into her sweet little girl's face?

Joanna's eyes were the same color as Abigail's. Her nose was a sweet button of a thing that reminded Abigail of her youngest *schweschder*. She ran a hand across the top of her *boppli*'s head. Soft hair the color of her own but with a bit more curl to it— that would be from Asher. His hair always did curl a little.

A nurse took Baby Jo long enough to swaddle her in a blanket—white with a little ribbon of pink and blue. "Her five-minute Apgar is a solid eight."

Abigail must have read about what that meant, but she couldn't think of it. The doctor picked up the baby, ran her finger-tips over the child's brow and then laid her in the crook of Abigail's arm.

"What is an Apgar score?"

"It's a test to assure us your *boppli* is doing well, and she is."

Abigail might have drifted off while she was holding her, because the next thing she knew *Mammi* was in the room, cooing over the baby. "You did a *wunderbaar* job, Abigail. I expected they would call me back to be with you, but apparently things went so fast there was no time. That's a real blessing, to have a quick birth."

"Isn't she beautiful?"

"She is that and more." *Mammi* bent and kissed the top of Jo's head. "May *Gotte*'s blessing be upon you, little one, all the days of your life."

"I've named her Joanna, but I think I'll call her Little Jo or maybe Baby Jo, at least while she's small enough to tolerate it."

They spoke for a few more minutes, and then a nurse came in and asked if she could eat something. Surprisingly, Abigail found that she was hungry. She ate well when they brought her scrambled eggs, toast and juice.

Mammi held Little Jo as Abigail ate, and that image of the dear old woman holding the newborn filled Abigail's heart with joy. *Gotte* had been *gut* to her. He'd seen her through a difficult time, and now she had so much to look forward to.

Joanna learning to walk.

Joanna saying her name.

Joanna going to school, working in a bakery or a shop, courting and marrying.

"Crying is normal," *Mammi* murmured. "Lots of emotions when a *boppli* is born."

She pushed away the plate of food, her appetite suddenly gone. "I was thinking of her marrying."

"That's a ways off."

"Yes, I suppose in one way it is. But in another way, it's just around the corner."

"It's *gut* to appreciate every day," *Mammi* agreed. She proceeded to guide Abigail in nursing Baby Jo, and after that they changed her diaper.

Abigail's heart flooded with joy as she cared for her child. She felt happier and more satisfied than any other day in her life.

As *Mammi* helped her to position Little Jo back in the crook of her arm, there was a tap on the door and Thomas stepped into the room.

* * *

Thomas couldn't take his eyes off Abigail. She was okay. Better than okay. She was sitting up and smiling. She looked—well, she looked positively radiant. Her auburn hair flowed around her shoulders. It reminded him of the other time he'd seen her without her *kapp,* when she'd been so sick and in danger of losing the baby. It seemed like yesterday and a lifetime ago all at the same time. He couldn't think clearly, only that she was here, and she was fine.

"Come meet my *doschder.*"

Thomas's gaze dropped to the bundle in her arms. He could just make out a little pink face. Stepping closer, it felt as if the world tilted slightly. His heart caught in his throat. He tried to speak, found he couldn't, swallowed and tried again.

"She's beautiful, Abigail."

"Isn't she? I know all mothers think so, but...to me, she's perfect."

Mammi clapped her hands. "All *Gotte*'s

creatures are beautiful and all are perfectly formed."

Standing, she tugged her purse strap up over her shoulder. "I'll go and put a call in to Naomi and Luke. Let them know that there's no need to rush up here. Mom and baby will soon be sleeping."

"Are you tired?" Thomas nearly slapped his own forehead. "Of course, you're tired. I should go..."

"Stay a few minutes, at least long enough to say hello."

Mammi slipped from the room, and Thomas dropped into the chair that she had been sitting in. Reaching out a finger, he stroked the baby's cheek. Had he ever seen anything so tiny and perfect and precious?

"Thomas, meet Joanna. And Joanna, this is Thomas. He's your..." She glanced up at him, then dropped her eyes back to the baby. "He will always be your very special friend. He drove us to the hospital."

"I'm surprised I didn't go the wrong direction."

"Were you rattled?"

"Rattled? After *Mammi*'s call, I put my coat on over my bedclothes, then had to run back inside and change."

They both laughed.

"She's okay? I know your due date was actually next week."

"It was. Or they thought it was, but the doctor said that Jo is perfect. She weighs six pounds, three ounces. Can you believe it?"

Thomas could believe it. He'd caught bigger fish than that. He glanced up at the clock. The hour had crept into the next day. It was Tuesday, the sixteenth of November.

He was still leaning forward, his hand resting on top of Abigail's bundle of joy. He knew he should sit back, keep his distance, but in that moment of new birth and fresh beginnings, the pull of the two of them was simply too strong. "'Tuesday's child is full of grace,'" he murmured.

"What's that?"

"Something my *mamm* used to say to each of us."

Her hand was beside his, as if she needed to stay very close to the baby, as if they were still attached by some emotional umbilical cord. He traced the back of her hand with his index finger, and her gaze jerked up to meet his—but she didn't pull away.

"I'd forgotten all about it." He cleared his throat, swallowed past the swell of emotions. "'Monday's child is fair of face, Tuesday's child is full of grace...'"

"That's beautiful." Abigail smiled, and suddenly Thomas was holding her hand between both of his. She tilted her head. "What's the rest of it?"

"'*Wednesday's child is full of woe.*'"

"Oh, that's true. I have a *bruder* born on a Wednesday. He's very dramatic."

Thomas laughed. He felt suddenly lightheaded, his heart unaccountably filled with joy. How had he gone from being a confirmed bachelor to losing his heart? And Abigail was acting as if there was nothing surprising about it. They were having a completely normal conversation as he sat there holding her hand, Abigail's newborn babe lying on the bed between them.

But there was nothing normal about it, because his world had been turned upside down.

"And Thursday?"

"Thursday?"

Abigail smiled at him as if he'd just said something very clever. "Thursday's child…"

"Oh. Right. 'Thursday's child has far to go.' I have no idea what that means."

"Friday's child…"

"'Is loving and giving.'"

Thomas didn't want this moment to end. He wanted to sit there, not worrying about the future or the past, and just revel in this moment with Abigail. Then she blushed, and he knew what she was about to say.

"I was born on a Friday."

"I should have guessed as much." Thomas shook his head. "I can't believe I remember this. If you'd asked me yesterday, I wouldn't have been able to tell you a word of it. Funny the things that come back to you during important moments."

Her eyes met his. He swallowed again and focused all of his energies on not leaning forward to kiss her. "Where were we?"

"Saturdays." She narrowed her eyes. "Say, what day were you born?"

"I was born on a Saturday, actually."

"And the saying?"

"'Saturday's child works hard for his living.'"

"You're making that up."

"*Nein*, I'm not."

"I might need to see it in writing—not your writing, but in a proper book."

He laughed. How was it that he could feel so lighthearted around her? Perhaps it was the lack of sleep, or the intensity of the moment. He shouldn't put too much weight on whatever was happening between them. He shouldn't put his faith in it.

"Don't leave me in suspense. What about Sunday?"

He rubbed his chin. "I can't seem to remember…"

"You do too! Now you're just teasing."

Baby Jo stirred, and Abigail pulled her

hand from his in order to adjust the blanket around her child.

Reluctantly, Thomas sat back, his eyes locked on the newborn. "'The child that is born on the Sabbath day is fair and wise and good in every way.'"

That sat between them for a moment, and then they both said simultaneously, *"Mammi."*

"We'll have to ask her." Abigail yawned.

"You should sleep."

"I am suddenly, deliciously tired. Can you set her in the bassinet, then push it closer to the bed?"

He didn't want to. He did not want to pick up that little bundle of joy, but he saw his arms reaching for her, then he was holding something so small and so amazing, that all other thoughts fled.

How could this have been in Abigail's body just a few hours ago? Baby Jo stared back at him, and that moment was Thomas's undoing. He lost his heart. He lost it to this child, this woman and this moment. He knew he'd never have another experience quite like it, even if they were to marry and have a dozen children.

Wait. What was he thinking?

Marry?

Have a dozen children?

He glanced around for the bassinet, placed Joanna gently in it and pushed the bed closer to Abigail. His pulse was thundering and his hands were sweating. He suddenly needed to be outside in the fresh air. He needed to be out of this room.

Abigail failed to notice his discomfort. Her eyes were on her child. She turned on her side, her hair spilling over her shoulder, snugged the hospital blanket up to her chin and yawned.

"I should go."

She nodded as her eyes drifted shut.

He'd reached the door when she said, "*Danki*, Thomas."

A dozen responses flitted through his mind.

No need to thank me.

Don't depend on me. I'm not reliable!

I love you, Abigail. I love you both.

But he didn't say any of those things. He whispered the age-old words, *"Gem gschehne,"* and then he practically ran from the room.

Chapter Ten

The next two weeks passed with a flurry. For Thanksgiving, Abigail, Baby Jo and *Mammi* went to the bishop's. Abigail was happy to be out of the house, and the Fishers' place was beginning to feel like a second home to her. Luke, Naomi and all of their children made a fuss over the baby, and though much of her situation was still unresolved, Abigail found herself thankful for the small things—a home, a healthy child, her church community, *Mammi*, Thomas.

November turned to December, and Abigail's thoughts turned to Christmas.

Her *boppli*'s first Christmas.

She wanted it to be special.

She wanted it to be amazing.

She wanted to talk to Thomas about her plans, but Thomas was avoiding her. She'd suspected as much the first week home, but now she was certain of it. Was it because of what had happened between them in the hospital room? Something had happened. He'd held her hand for a full five minutes, and his eyes—his eyes had said what he refused to admit, that he cared about her.

At least she thought he did.

She hoped he did.

But how was she to know when she never saw him? He rarely came into the house anymore, and the few times he did he avoided sitting down, avoided being alone with Abigail and absolutely refused to hold Baby Jo.

The last time Abigail had tried to pass the *boppli* to him still caused her to laugh—and sigh. *Mammi* had been taking a nap, and Abigail needed to fetch a clean diaper. It was one of the rare times that Thomas was in the house. He was describing her options for spring crops. How could he be worried about spring crops in December? He was waving a seed catalog around when Baby Jo had begun to fuss.

Abigail stood and tried to put the *boppli* in his arms. Thomas had held his hands up in front of him and taken two steps back. Two giant steps. Like in that old game Mother May I.

"Oh, my, you won't break her."

"But I could."

"Thomas, be serious."

"I am serious. I have a hard-and-fast rule that I don't cuddle, touch or carry babies until they can hold their own head up."

Abigail sighed. "Then sit here on the couch beside her while I go and fetch some clean diapers and a warm cloth."

She placed the child in a cocoon of pillows on the couch, then turned toward Thomas and cocked her head. "Unless you want to change her?"

"For sure and certain I do not." His voice was grave, but his expression had softened.

She wanted to reach out and touch his face, to ask him what had happened between them and why he was afraid. But Jo scrunched up her face and let out a healthy wail. Thomas looked as if the mare had bolted over the fence.

"Don't panic. I'll hurry." By the time she made it back into the sitting room, Thomas was patting Jo's stomach and saying "Whoa, baby. Whoa…" in a gentle voice.

"She's not a horse, you know."

"I guess."

"You guess?"

"I know she's not a horse, Abigail, but sometimes what works with an animal works with a person."

She started to set him straight on that but decided now probably wasn't the time. At least he was talking to her. "My *mamm* arrives next week."

"I know you're looking forward to that."

"Not really." She sighed. "I should be. I've been speaking to *Mammi* and Luke about it. I want to have a *gut* visit with her, but my *mamm* is…difficult. It's easier for me to avoid any confrontation with her, so I tend to find myself holding my tongue and fleeing the room."

"Hmm."

"Hmm what?"

"You've never done that with me."

She unpinned Jo's diaper. Thomas made a face and pulled away. "That's worse than what you clean out of a horse stable."

"It is not!"

"Wow. Big things come from little packages."

She folded up the diaper and handed it to him. "Can you put this in the pail in the bathroom? I'll deal with it later."

Thomas held the diaper as if it was filled with toxic sludge.

Abigail picked up Baby Jo, who was much happier with her clean diaper. "Your *onkel* Thomas is silly," she whispered.

"*Onkel* Thomas, huh?"

She hadn't realized he was back. She smiled up at him sweetly. "You're sort of like an *onkel*."

"I guess."

It was an awkward moment. Did he want to be more? Did he want to be less? She simply couldn't read his thoughts so she opted to change the subject.

"Say, Thomas, I've been thinking about Christmas."

"Have you now?" He perched on the edge of the rocking chair, as if he might need to dash from the room at any moment.

"I was thinking that I'd like the holiday to be extra special for Jo. Her first Christmas should be unforgettable. I'd like this room to be filled with the sights and smells of Christmas. I know I don't have much money…"

Her voice trailed off as she thought of what an understatement that was. She'd had a call from the lawyer the day after coming home with Baby Jo. Gabriela Martinez had done a thorough analysis of Asher's finances and learned that he had borrowed heavily against the farm—to build the fences and acquire an additional section of land. Financially, things were looking grim. She'd shared the news with

Mammi and Thomas. *Mammi* has assured her *Gotte* was still in control. Thomas had grumbled something about people being irresponsible and stomped out to the barn.

"I actually have very little money, but I think there are a lot of things we can do that won't cost much."

"Planning on a Christmas tree?"

She tilted her head to the side and studied him, aware that he was teasing her. "*Nein*. No Christmas tree."

"Oh, I thought you were going all *Englisch* on me."

"Sure, *ya*. Maybe you could fetch me a plastic Santa or a herd of plastic reindeer to put on the lawn." When Thomas continued to stare at her, she continued. "I was thinking of putting some pine boughs on the windowsills. Perhaps you could bring up a small hay bale to the porch and I could decorate it like a snowman."

"Wait a few weeks. I'm sure we'll have snow. That always looks Christmassy."

She tried to ignore his teasing.

"If I could find some bushes with red berries, maybe bring a few of those branches inside." She looked down at the baby, who was now sound asleep. "I want her first Christmas to be extra special. I want every Christmas to be extra special."

Thomas popped out of the chair abruptly, pulling at the collar of his shirt as if the room were suddenly unbearably warm.

"What's wrong?"

"She's an infant, Abigail. She won't know if you've decorated for Christmas or not."

The skin over her right eye started to twitch—a sure sign she was about to lose her temper. "She might know. She could be forming memories right now."

"You're being silly."

"I am not." Now she was getting hot. She could feel the flush creeping up her cheeks.

"We're not *Englisch*."

"I never said we were!" She stood and put Baby Jo in her bassinet. Somehow the infant continued to sleep blissfully despite the loud conversation going on around her. Putting her hands on her hips, Abigail faced Thomas. "What's bugging you?"

"Nothing's bugging me."

"Plainly something is—you don't stop in to visit anymore, you never eat dinner with us and now you're making fun of my Christmas plans. What difference does it make to you what we do?"

"You're right." He snatched up his hat from the coffee table and squished it on his head. "It makes no difference to me at all."

And then he was gone.

Just like that.

She didn't know whether to laugh or cry. She did not understand men at all. But she was left with a profound sense of disappointment. She'd wanted him to join in her planning. She'd wanted him to be a part of their small Christmas celebration.

At dinner that night, she broached the subject of Thomas with *Mammi*. She was grateful that the dear woman was still staying with her. A few days after she'd come home with Jo, she'd asked *Mammi* if she needed to get back to her own place.

Mammi had smiled and said, "I'm in no hurry, as long as you'll have me."

They felt like a family, the three of them.

Abigail wanted *Mammi* there, and she most certainly wanted her there when her *mamm* came to visit. But that wasn't the first concern on her mind as they ate chicken and dumplings.

"Thomas seems rather put out with me lately."

"Does he now?"

"I know you've noticed that he rarely eats with us anymore."

"I suppose he's quite busy taking care of this place. There's a lot of work for a farmer to do in the winter. Most people don't realize that."

"Oh, I realize, but he found time before..." She stirred her spoon around in her bowl, found another piece of chicken and popped it into her mouth.

"Before when, dear?"

"Before Jo was born." She was remembering the feel of his hand holding hers that night in the hospital. She was thinking of the look on his face as he'd moved Baby Jo from Abigail's hospital bed to the bassinet. His expression had been one of tenderness, of wonder, of love. "He loves Jo. I know he does."

"We all love her—she's a sweet blessing from the Lord."

"I think he's afraid." She picked up her knife, sliced off a sliver of butter and spread it across her muffin. Waving the knife back and forth, she added, "He's afraid of getting close. To me or Jo. I'm just sure that's what it is. Either that or... or he doesn't care as much as I thought."

"Sometimes caring can be frightening."

"What do you mean?"

"Well, if you don't care and someone rejects you, then it doesn't really matter. But if you do care, then that rejection hurts."

"Baby Jo wouldn't reject him. She loves everyone. Did you see the way she smiled at Luke yesterday?"

"Could have been gas."

"Maybe, but I prefer to think she knows his voice. And she watches things now.

This morning I was sweeping the floor, and her eyes were following me back and forth across the room."

"Before you know it, she'll be doing chores with you."

Abigail sighed and ate another spoonful of the dumplings. "I'll be honest with you, *Mammi*. I'd thought...that is to say, I'd hoped...that Thomas was beginning to care. Not just for Jo, but for me."

She felt silly saying it out loud.

What if she'd just been imagining things between them?

But *Mammi* was now smiling like a child on Christmas morning.

"Did he say something to you?" Abigail asked. "About me?"

"Sometimes it's not what a person says so much as the way he acts that portrays his feelings."

"And the way he's acting is strange."

"Marriages are made in heaven—but then so are thunder and lightning."

"Another proverb? Really?"

"Just something my *dat* used to say

whenever he and my *mamm* would be at odds with one another."

Abigail sighed. "My parents didn't speak when they were fighting, which, looking back, I think was much of the time."

"Perhaps tomorrow you should go out to the barn."

"I should go to the barn?"

"You know, it would do you *gut* to get some exercise, and some time away from Baby Jo wouldn't hurt."

"I don't need time away."

Mammi forged ahead as if Abigail hadn't spoken at all. "If Thomas won't come to lunch, you can take lunch to Thomas." Then she looked up and winked.

Which made Abigail laugh, and then *Mammi* was laughing, and then Jo was looking from one to the other and waving her little hands.

Life was *gut*, Abigail realized.

Even though men were not to be understood.

Still, the lunch idea wasn't a bad one.

The next morning, she opened her eyes

and realized she felt better than she had in a week. Why did the day seem brighter? Jo had still awakened her twice in the night to nurse, but Abigail didn't feel one bit tired. Then she remembered *Mammi*'s advice, and she knew that her mood was improved because she had a plan.

It was best to be honest with herself.

She had feelings for Thomas Albrecht. If he returned her feelings, then it was time to know that. And if he didn't, then she'd proceed to read up on old maids and learn how to be one.

The morning flew by. She did some housework, some knitting and even a little reading. The baby book said she should give Jo supervised tummy time so she could practice raising her head. Abigail placed her on an old quilt that *Mammi* had brought, and her *doschder* pushed out her arms and legs as if she were swimming.

Before Abigail knew it, her stomach was growling, and Baby Jo had gone down for her late-morning nap.

Mammi cut thick slices of ham, placed

it on fresh bread and wrapped the entire thing in a dish towel. Abigail added a plastic container of oatmeal-raisin cookies and a thermos of coffee.

"Off I go."

"I would wish you good luck, but I don't think luck has anything to do with this." As an afterthought, *Mammi* added, "Don't hurry back!"

Thomas wasn't looking forward to the sandwich he'd brought for lunch. Peanut butter was *gut*, but a man occasionally needed something more substantial. No doubt *Mammi* and Abigail were having a nice hot lunch. He thought of going inside, but immediately rejected the idea.

He'd vowed to keep his distance from Abigail.

The last thing she needed at this point was to be saddled with a man like him. She had enough problems, and he couldn't possibly be that selfish as to wish himself and his history on her.

He sat in Asher's office, in the corner of

the barn, stewing over the future. As he worked oil into Belle's harness, he wondered who would take care of Abigail's mare when he no longer worked for her. How long was he going to work here? She'd shared with him that she had returned the lawyer's phone calls twice. Gabriela had sounded optimistic that the estate would be settled soon, though soon to a lawyer might be different than it was to a single mom.

He was thinking of how few options Abigail had, when she appeared in the doorway. He stared at her with his mouth slightly ajar, then remembered his *mamm* saying, "You'll catch a fly if you leave your mouth open."

He shut his mouth.

"I brought you lunch." She held up a basket that looked as if it held enough food for two.

"Oh. Um… *Danki.*" He glanced around the room, determined to look anywhere but at the woman standing in the doorway. She was wearing a dark blue frock with a matching apron. Her cheeks were red from the cold and strands of her auburn hair had escaped from her *kapp*. She looked fresh and young and vibrant. She looked beautiful.

He pushed stuff into a pile in the center of the desk. "I guess you can just leave it there on the edge."

"Leave it? I came out to eat with you."

Thomas stared at her, then clamped his mouth shut again.

"You look awfully surprised."

"I don't think you've left Jo before."

"*Nein*, but *Mammi*'s there, of course. She says it would do me *gut* to get a little exercise, and that time away from the baby is important."

"Oh." Seeing that she was going to sit in the only other chair, he jumped up and moved it closer to the desk, then turned up the small gas heater because the room was rather cold. He shut the door to the office so the heat would build up, then wondered if he should shut it or leave it open.

He didn't want to make Abigail uncomfortable.

She was already unpacking the lunch and glanced up in time to say, "*Ya,* I think shutting the door will help. I didn't realize it's so cold."

"December in Indiana." What a stupid thing to say! She knew it was December. She'd been talking about Christmas the previous day. His thoughts were all over the place. This was Abigail. They'd been working together for more than two months. He needed to calm down.

He stuck his hands in his pockets, then pulled them back out and crossed his arms. That didn't feel right either. Where did he normally put his hands? Why was he feeling so awkward?

Then he spied the ham sandwiches she was unwrapping.

"Those look better than my peanut butter sandwich."

"I like peanut butter on summer days, but in the winter, I want something a little more substantial."

Exactly what he was thinking. He sat across from her, then cleaned off more of the desk by dumping the things that had piled up there into a box on the floor.

She pushed a sandwich toward him. Wagging the thermos back and forth, she asked, "Do you have another cup?"

He did. Though it wasn't quite clean. He rinsed it out in the small sink, then set it in front of her. She poured steaming coffee into the mug, then poured some for herself into the lid of the thermos.

He nearly groaned when he took the first bite of the sandwich.

"Hungry?"

"I'm pretty sure I was in danger of starving." He forced himself to slow down, but was happy to see she'd brought two sandwiches for him and one for herself. "Hungrier than I realized."

"Must be hard, being a bachelor and all. I don't suppose you have much time for cooking."

"True, but Mary Lehman—she and her husband own the mercantile below my apartment—Mary sends over dinners most nights. She spoils me, actually."

"I should meet her sometime." Abigail smiled and wiggled her eyebrows. "You talk about her like she's family."

"She is." He proceeded to tell her about Mary and John and their children. He recounted how they'd met, then admitted that the two had become like surrogate parents to him.

Abigail sighed heavily as she finished her sandwich. "Speaking of family, my *mamm* arrives next week."

"Anything I can do?"

"*Ya.* Sure. If you'd don a dress and *kapp,* sneak into the house and pretend to be me for the next week, that would be great."

Thomas rubbed his jawline. "My five-o'clock shadow might give me away."

Abigail nodded in agreement, then popped the lid off the plastic container.

He rubbed his stomach and groaned.

"Too full?"

"*Nein.* I am never too full for *Mammi*'s oatmeal cookies."

"I'll have you know I made these."

"Did you, now?"

"I can cook and bake."

"Hidden talents."

Instead of being offended, she laughed. "I guess I haven't done much of anything since you've met me—except for feeling sorry for myself. I've turned that into a real skill set."

"Don't be so hard on yourself, Abigail." His gaze met hers, and he remembered the feel of her hand in his. He thought of her and Baby Jo mere hours after her birth. Had he really shared that experience with them? And he expected to be able to run from his feelings? He was a fool.

"You look suddenly serious."

"Abigail, there's something I need to say to you."

"There is?"

"I'm sorry I've been avoiding you."

"I knew it!"

He couldn't help smiling. She looked so proud of herself, as if she'd cracked a big mystery. "I haven't meant to be rude."

"You hurt my feelings, Thomas. I thought we were—friends. I thought maybe we were...we were more than that."

It would help if she would stare down at her hands, but she didn't. Nope. Abigail wasn't going to let him off the hook that easily. She watched him and waited, until the silence grew uncomfortable and he was tempted to spill all the secrets of his heart. She didn't need to know all of that, though. She had enough problems of her own without wrestling with his past, with the possibility that he'd become a drunken Amish farmer.

He cleared his throat. "I didn't mean to hurt your feelings, but there are reasons that I don't think it would be in your best interest to get close to me."

"Maybe that's for me to decide." Her voice was gentle but firm. It surprised him. The distraught young widow who had been unable to shoo a goat off her front porch had turned into a confident woman. When had that happened?

"I don't... I don't know how to do this."

His appetite vanished. He set the oatmeal cookie down, pushed it away. "I don't know how to be your friend, or be more than your friend, and not risk hurting you."

"Is that what's bothering you?" To his horror, she popped up out of the chair and walked around to his side of the desk. Leaning her backside against it, she crossed her arms, looked down at him and smiled. "You're not going to hurt me, Thomas. You're a *gut* man. I can trust you."

"But..."

"And even though you're afraid of newborns, you're very *gut* with Jo."

"I am?"

"She wants to see you more."

"She does?"

"A mother can tell."

"Oh."

"You'll come inside for dinner tonight?"

When he hesitated, she added, "I'm sure Mary will understand if you don't need her leftovers for one evening."

The thought of going into the snug little

house, sitting at the kitchen table and eating with Abigail and *Mammi* and Baby Jo lifted his spirits more than he would have thought possible.

"*Ya*. Okay. That sounds *gut*."

"Friends?" She held her small hand out to him in a distinctly *Englisch* fashion.

He laughed and shook it. "Okay, friends."

"And maybe more."

Before he realized what she intended to do, Abigail leaned forward and kissed him softly on the lips. While he was trying to figure out what he thought about that, she pulled away and walked out of the office, out of the barn and headed back to the house. Thomas was left staring at a container full of cookies and a half-empty thermos of coffee.

He could still taste Abigail's lips, and her words echoed in his ears.

Friends...and maybe more.

Chapter Eleven

Abigail's *mamm* had been visiting for four days, and Abigail had taken to hiding in the barn. She wasn't proud of that, but she reasoned that a person should do what they needed to do.

Thomas walked into the office, smiled at her and dropped his hat onto the desk. "I'd love to believe that you're out here to see me, but I take it your *mamm* is on a tear again."

"This morning it was about Jo's name."

"Is that so?"

"Yup. Apparently, I named my child wrong."

"Huh."

Abigail shrugged her shoulders. "Tomorrow, she goes home, so I just need to hang out in here..." she glanced up at the clock "...twenty-two more hours."

Thomas couldn't help laughing. He stopped next to the chair she was sitting in, leaned down and kissed her. Abigail thought that Thomas's kisses were one of the sweetest moments of her day.

And to think it was all because she'd been brave enough to kiss him first.

She didn't know where this was headed, and she wasn't particularly worried about it. She'd never properly courted, and she thought she might actually enjoy doing so with Thomas. Abigail understood now that being with a person, spending time with them, sharing your problems with them, watching a sunset with them—those things all told you more about a person than a letter received once a week.

Though she'd love to have a letter from Thomas. Perhaps she could ask him to write her.

Thomas pulled away, then kissed Baby Jo on the forehead.

"Want to hold her?" Abigail teased.

"Uh-uh. Not yet. Maybe when she starts walking."

"Hey. I thought you were waiting until she could hold her head up."

"That and walk and maybe drive a buggy."

"Wow. You are afraid of children."

"I prefer the word cautious."

She proceeded to talk about her Christmas plans. Thomas still didn't seem on board with that, but she thought he would eventually come around. Besides, it was her house for another few weeks at least. She could do whatever she wanted until the judge declared a final ruling on the farm and house and Asher's debts.

Abigail was tempted to sink into despair over her financial situation, and there were times that she did. Occasionally, she fell asleep with tears on her pillow. Once in a while, she took to the porch with the broom to work off her anxiety. But overall, she was coming around to *Mammi*'s way of thinking—*Gotte* would provide.

She pushed away her dark thoughts about the future. There wasn't a single thing she could do about any of those things, and she refused to ruin a fine December afternoon pretending that she could. Instead, she favored Thomas with a detailed description of her Christmas decorating plans.

He interrupted her discussion of the merits of pine boughs over cedar boughs. "Talk to me seriously for a minute. How is it going with your *mamm*?"

"I was serious before. I'd stay here in the barn until she leaves if I could."

"Abigail, that's not healthy."

"I think it's very healthy. If you see a hurricane coming toward you, the wise thing to do is get out of the way. That's what I'm doing."

Thomas sat back in his chair, causing it to squeak, and steepled his fingers together. She knew that look. He was going to lecture her.

"Don't even start. You've barely spent

any time with her. In fact, have you even been in the house in the last week? *Nein,* you stay safely out here in the peaceful serenity of the barn." She glanced around, wondering if she could hide here until her mother left. When Thomas cleared his throat, she added, "You have no idea what it's like to live with her."

"But you're not living with her. She's visiting. Your time with her is limited. I just wish you could enjoy it."

"Last night she corrected my knitting."

"So?"

"She doesn't know how to knit."

Thomas laughed, but Abigail didn't see the humor in the situation.

"She also mopped the kitchen floor, when plainly I had just mopped it."

"Odd."

"And she treats Jo exactly like..." She would not cry. She might still have mommy hormones raging through her system, but she was not a child! "She treats Jo like she treated me—efficiently but without any outward affection."

"Explain to me what you mean." His voice was soft and his eyes compassionate.

A little of Abigail's defensiveness slipped away.

"If *Mammi* holds Jo, she'll kiss her on the head, or smell her neck, or speak to her in a singsong voice. You even get a goofy grin when you're letting her clutch your finger." He didn't deny it, so she pushed on. "And when I hold her it feels as if a piece of my heart is finally reattached to my body."

"But…"

"But when my *mamm* holds her, it's as if she's holding a piece of laundry or a recipe book. She's detached. She doesn't even smile. She doesn't smell her or kiss her."

That confession sat between them for a moment.

"She did travel a long way to be here. I have to believe your *mamm* loves Jo, and I believe she loves you."

Abigail shrugged. "She doesn't act like it."

"Look." Thomas sat forward and waited

until she met his gaze. "You don't have unlimited time with your parents. I made that mistake with my *dat* and *mamm*—and now they're both gone. If you have something to say to your mother, then say it. Be an adult, Abigail. Don't hide in a barn in order to avoid an uncomfortable situation."

She thought the top of her head might pop off.

"How dare you…"

"How dare I? Maybe I dare because I care about you, and I don't like to see you tearing yourself up about a family relationship."

"You make me so mad." She jumped up and started bundling Jo back into her coat and mittens and blanket.

"Do you plan to run away every time you get mad?"

"I am not running away. In case you forgot, I live here. This is *my* barn and that is *my* house." She waved in the direction of the house in case he was still confused.

"For now." Thomas's words came across solemn, quiet, pointed.

"You don't need to remind me that I might lose everything, Thomas. Just like you don't need to imply that I'm a terrible *doschder*. I'm well aware of both things." She stormed out of the barn, forgetting her outer bonnet and her gloves so that she had to sprint back to the house. There wasn't any snow yet, nothing to brighten the day, just wind and clouds and cold.

The afternoon passed slowly.

After dinner, Abigail listened to her mother and *Mammi* discuss the best home remedies for various ailments.

Tea made from a daisy-type plant called feverfew and mixed with honey helped a cold.

Peeled ginger root eased the pain of teething.

Peppermint-flavored water relieved colic.

Abigail was immensely grateful that no one had a cold, Jo wasn't teething yet and her child had absolutely no sign of colic. Still, *Mammi* and her mother seemed to enjoy discussing various ailments.

It was impossible to sit in the same room

and not compare the two women. Abigail's *mamm* sat on the couch—ramrod straight—rarely smiled and spoke in grim declarations. *Mammi* was burrowed into a chair with several pillows positioned next to her and a shawl around her shoulders. She smiled frequently, laughed occasionally and her words had a singsong quality to them.

She couldn't imagine two more different people.

Abigail remembered Thomas's accusation and got mad all over again. She wasn't avoiding an uncomfortable conversation. There was no point in even having such a thing.

Someone cannot show what they haven't learned.

Abigail wanted to slap her hands over her ears to block out *Mammi*'s words, but they'd been spoken to her weeks ago—before Jo was even born. They existed now only in her heart. She couldn't block that out.

Someone cannot show what they haven't learned.

It might be true. She was willing to admit that. But did it excuse how her *mamm* behaved? Could Abigail possibly let her off the hook so easily? She suddenly remembered the Scripture that Luke had preached from the Sunday before. He'd quoted from the first book of Corinthians, the thirteenth chapter—what Abigail thought of as the marriage chapter.

Love is patient. Love is kind.

She certainly wasn't being either of those things toward her mother.

Love does not dishonor.

Was she dishonoring her mother?

It keeps no record of wrongs.

And that's where she knew she had failed. She did keep a record of wrongs. She remembered every time her mother had said a sharp word or denied a request or stepped away from an embrace.

"I think I will go to bed early tonight." *Mammi* tucked her knitting into her basket and stood. She kissed the baby, wished Abigail's *mamm* a good evening and pulled Abigail into a hug.

She didn't say anything else.

She didn't need to.

Abigail tried to work on the tiny sweater she was making for Jo, but she kept knitting where she was supposed to purl, and increasing where she was supposed to decrease. Finally, she set the project aside, went to the kitchen and fetched two cups of herbal tea.

While she was there, she prayed that she'd have the right words to speak with her *mamm*.

She walked back into the sitting room, placed the mug of hot tea next to her *mamm* and sat in the chair across from her. "I want to thank you for coming."

"There's no need to thank me. I was eager to meet my newest *grandkinner.*"

That was a surprise to Abigail. She certainly didn't look eager. Did her *mamm* not know how to allow her expression to mirror her feelings? Abigail shook away the thought. She needed to stay focused if she was going to make it through this conversation.

"I also want to apologize."

Her mother gave her a very clear what-have-you-done-now look.

"I'm afraid that I haven't honored you in the way I should. I've... I've kept a record of wrongs—or perceived wrongs. And I think those things, those thoughts, stand between us. They build this unsurmountable wall that I don't know how to find my way around."

Her mother sighed, as if vexed by her confession, but she didn't look up from her darning. She didn't knit or crochet, but she could darn better than anyone Abigail knew.

"You're too sensitive, Abigail. You always have been."

"*Ya*. Maybe so."

"In my day, we didn't have time to sit around and worry about our feelings. Life was harder then." She glanced up, only to stare out the front window. It was too dark to see anything, but still her gaze remained there. "Perhaps it was better, when life was harder. There was less time to sit and worry over what someone said, or how they said it, or what they didn't say."

"*Ya*, maybe so," Abigail repeated, though she didn't believe that. She thought that no matter how busy your hands were, your thoughts could still toss worries and joys back and forth. That was human nature. Wasn't it?

"Soon Joanna will be up and running around. You'll remarry and have more children, and then you'll be too busy for such foolishness."

A silence fell between them as Abigail puzzled over her mother's reaction. Is that what had happened to her mother? Had someone told her she was foolish for having feelings? Had they ridiculed her or corrected her or scolded her in a way that changed her behavior permanently?

Abigail finished her tea and stood to retrieve the cups. She took them to the kitchen, washed them and set them in the drainer. It was when she paused between the two rooms that she noticed her mother staring down at Baby Jo—a look of pure wonder on her face.

When she noticed Abigail standing there, watching, she schooled her face, sat straighter and reached for another sock to darn.

But the moment had happened.

Abigail hadn't imagined it.

She walked across the room and sat on the couch next to her mother, closer than she had been before. "*Danki, Mamm.* For taking care of me. For providing for us. I know you and *Dat* did the best that you could—and because you did, I'm here today. I'm able to take care of Jo. *Danki* for taking the long bus ride from Colorado to Indiana and for staying with us. I love you and *Dat*, and I appreciate you both."

Her mother looked up, and for a fleeting moment the stoic look was replaced with one of tenderness. It didn't last. She tsked, reached out and felt Abigail's head, then resumed her darning. "You sound feverish. Perhaps you're getting a cold. You should go to bed early too."

"I will, *Mamm*." Abigail reached over and squeezed her mother's hand. Wonder of wonders, she didn't pull away.

It wasn't much, but it was a start.

Someone cannot show what they haven't learned.

Perhaps, in matters of the heart, mothers could learn from their daughters.

Later, while Abigail was tossing in bed, she realized that she was no longer angry with her *mamm*. It was simply too exhausting to carry around that much anger, that many old hurts.

So why was she tossing?

Why couldn't she sleep?

It was Thomas's fault. The way he looked at her so smugly, the advice that he tossed around like seedsto the birds. And to think that he wouldn't even hold her *doschder* in his arms. He made her so mad!

Did she want to build her future with a man like that?

What was she thinking? He'd said nothing about the future.

What did it matter that they'd shared a

few kisses, a few walks in the fields, several mugs of hot chocolate? No promises had been exchanged. No confessions of love.

On one level Abigail knew that she was being unreasonable, moody even. Just hours ago, she'd thought about how nice it was to court someone, that it didn't bother her not knowing where they'd stand tomorrow. She'd been lying to herself.

That uncertainty did bother her because nothing in her life was assured.

Except *Mammi*.

And her parents.

And her faith.

She'd cling to those things, and—for a while at least—leave courting out of the equation.

Thomas knew he'd stepped into a pile of manure, figuratively speaking. He'd gone over the conversation with Mary Lehman, and then with his *schweschder* Lily. Both had stared at him in amazement and asked if he'd lost his mind.

"Do you want to be a bachelor forever?" Lily had asked, then proceeded to beat a rug rather too aggressively.

Mary had simply pushed a tin of brownies into his hands and suggested he share them with Abigail. "Sometimes chocolate can mend the heart."

He hadn't done anything wrong.

Abigail had needed to hear what he'd said.

Then he realized that he wouldn't have wanted to hear those words five or ten years ago. No one could have advised him on his relationship with his parents. He'd been dealing with too many feelings, too much history.

Why did he think that he could correct Abigail and set her on the straight path? How arrogant of him.

He'd shown up at her door late the next afternoon and offered the tin of brownies.

"What's this?"

"Chocolate. I hear it's a good remedy for saying stupid things."

"As is an apology."

"I'm sorry, Abigail." He meant it too. He hadn't wanted to cause her more trouble, more pain. He'd wanted to help, but he'd made a mess of it. "Forgive me?"

She'd squeezed her eyes shut and tried to hold back a smile, but she was only successful for a moment. "You might as well come in and try some of these."

They'd sat at the kitchen table, Jo in the baby carrier that sat on top of a high chair. She'd waved her arms enthusiastically when he'd walked into the room.

"I told you she enjoys your visits."

Thomas almost groaned. He was a goner. When he wasn't with Abigail and Jo, they were all he could think about. When he was with them, he wanted to stay. Why was he fighting this?

Because of his family history. Because he cared about them.

But maybe, just possibly, they could overcome that.

Did he dare to hope as much?

Mammi walked into the room and clapped her hands together. "Brownies. I love brownies."

She'd sat at the table and joined them. The three talked about the lawyer—they still hadn't heard any updates—and Christmas, which was ten days away, and Abigail's mom. The visit had ended on a better note than Abigail had expected.

Abigail told *Mammi* and Thomas about her conversation with her *mamm*.

"Relationships are fragile," *Mammi* said. "Handle with prayer." Her expression was uncharacteristically grave, but then she broke into a smile.

"Supper is almost ready, and now we've gone and eaten dessert first. I'd say that's a fine thing to do on a cold December afternoon. Why don't you two go and check on the animals while I slice some of the bread we baked? I'll have everything set out by the time you make your rounds."

Thomas knew the animals did not need to be checked on, and from the way Abigail looked at him, she knew it too. But they walked out to the barn, and they returned thirty minutes later hand in hand. Thomas could breathe again. He might be afraid of the future, but he would be a fool to succumb to that fear.

The next day was Sunday, and Abigail and Thomas sat together during the meal. He normally didn't attend her church service, because his own church met on the same weekends. But he'd wanted to be with her. He'd *needed* to be with her. Since he knew most of the people in her community, he'd felt immediately at home. And when he caught a few knowing smiles tossed their way, he didn't really care. In fact, he wanted people to know how he felt about Abigail.

On Monday, he wasn't able to go to Abigail's, as he'd promised to help his *bruder*-in-law with some roof repairs on his barn.

On Tuesday, he showed up at his regular time, but Abigail didn't come out at lunch. In fact, he hadn't seen her all morning. He plodded over to the house, knocked on the door, whacked the dirt off his boots and walked in.

Mammi was carrying a tray and Baby Jo was hollering loud enough to be heard from the barn.

"Let me take that." The tray had a bowl of soup that looked untouched, a mug of tea and some crackers. "What are you doing with this tray?"

"I was trying to tempt Abigail to eat, but to no avail." *Mammi* tottered into the kitchen and scooped Jo up from her bassinet. "I'm afraid that maybe we need to call the doctor."

"What's wrong?"

"Flu, maybe. I'm not sure." She moved Jo to her shoulder and rubbed her back in soft circles. "Can you go to the phone shack and call? Doc Amanda is still making house calls, as far as I know."

"Sure, *Mammi*. Of course I will."

The next few hours passed in a blur. Doc Amanda didn't make it out until after seven in the evening. Amanda was in her fifties, had short gray hair and had been caring for the Amish community in and around Shipshewana for years. After she'd examined Abigail, she sat at the kitchen table and accepted a cup of hot tea. "It's influenza, I'm sure. We'll have her test results back tomorrow, but in the meantime keep giving her aspirin to bring down the fever and push fluids on her."

Mammi pushed up her glasses. "What about Baby Jo? Should she be around Abigail?"

"She's already been exposed, as have you two." The doctor gulped down the rest of the tea and stood. "Watch for symptoms— fever, sore muscles, fatigue."

Thomas had been around Abigail a lot in the last week, and he felt fine. Maybe he was immune to the flu. "Can you give her any kind of medicine?"

Doc Amanda pulled a bottle of pills from her bag. "Twice a day for five days. And if anyone else comes down with it, I'll send more."

"What do we owe you?" *Mammi* asked.

The doctor waved her away. "I'm aware of Abigail's situation. There's no charge for the visit."

After she'd driven away, Thomas sat down at the table with *Mammi*. Finally, he said, "You can't handle a sick Abigail and an infant on your own."

"There was a day when I could have, but you're probably right. Perhaps we should call Naomi or Clare…"

"I'm going back to my place to grab a few changes of clothes." When she started to protest, he said, "I'm here every day anyway, *Mammi*. It makes the most sense. I'll sleep on the couch, and I can spell you a couple of hours in the morning, maybe an hour or two in the afternoon, and we can split the night up into shifts."

Mammi glanced left, then right, then around the table.

"They're on your head."

She smiled and tugged the glasses off the top of her head. When she'd pushed them firmly in place, she said simply, "*Gut* plan."

But Thomas didn't leave for his place immediately. First, he needed to see Abigail.

He walked back to her room, tapped on the door and then let himself in.

Abigail was curled on her side, reminding him of the time he'd sat beside her in the hospital. She coughed, winced and then tried to peer at him through half-closed eyes. He placed a hand on her forehead. She was burning up.

"Trying to avoid lunches in the barn?"

"*Ya*. You caught me." Her voice sounded like buggy wheels over gravel.

He winced and perched on the edge of the bed. "You're going to be okay, Abigail. *Mammi* and I, we'll take care of everything."

A healthy Abigail might have argued.

Instead, she drifted into an uneasy sleep, her breathing ragged and labored, broken occasionally by a harsh cough.

And Thomas wondered why he had ever

thought he could live without this woman. How had he been foolish enough to consider walking away? Looking at her now—sick, vulnerable, weak—he understood that his heart had already made the decision for him.

Now she needed to get well, so he could tell her.

Chapter Twelve

Abigail blinked her eyes and stared at the light coming through her bedroom windows. Why was she still in bed? What time was it? And where was Baby Jo?

Mammi's wizened face appeared smiling down at her.

"*Gut* to see you awake."

"What…?" She struggled to free herself from the covers, and *Mammi* helped her sit up. She plumped the pillows behind her, handed her a glass of water and then sat on the side of the bed.

"Baby Jo?"

"She's *gut*. Thomas bundled her up and took her out to the barn."

"Thomas has her?" The words came out as a croak.

"Ya." *Mammi*'s relaxed smile put Abigail at ease. "You've missed a few things since you took sick. Those two have bonded quite well."

"But he's afraid of babies."

"Indeed. Yet sometimes *Gotte* uses the thing we're most afraid of to remind us of His sovereignty." *Mammi* added, "Trust me. I know."

Abigail shook her head, studying the older woman who had become such a dear friend in a relatively short time. "What have you ever been afraid of?"

Mammi laughed, and the sound was merry and bright. "Mostly, I was afraid of being alone, but *Gotte* showed me that we're never truly alone. He's always with us, am I right? And He sends others to be with us, to be near us in our time of need."

Abigail thought of Thomas and *Mammi*, Clare, and Naomi and Luke. She had vague memories of each of them being there, sitting with her, praying for her.

"What day is it?"

"Monday, December twentieth."

"Christmas is...?"

"Saturday. Perhaps you were dreaming of a white Christmas, and that's why we received three inches of snow, plus there's more forecast for later in the week." *Mammi* picked up her knitting project— something Abigail didn't remember her working on before. The yarn was a soft lavender, which just happened to be Abigail's favorite color. "Baby Jo's first Christmas will be here before we know it."

Abigail was suddenly overwhelmed with the need to hold her *doschder*.

"Shower first," *Mammi* suggested, as if anticipating what she was about to say. "Then a light breakfast, and by that time Thomas should be back with Baby Jo. They go out there every day."

How long had she been sick? She remembered going to church with *Mammi* and Jo and Thomas. She remembered her *mamm* leaving the day before that. But anything between Sunday and waking this morning—an entire week apparently— was a blur. "Thomas cares for Jo by himself?"

"Indeed."

"A lot has certainly changed in the past week." She was thinking of how he'd been afraid to hold her *doschder*, of the look of panic on his face when she'd tried to settle Jo in his arms.

"They go out to the barn office every day from eight to ten, like clockwork. And before you start worrying, he does his paperwork in the barn office then. It's not as if he has her in the barn loft."

"I'm not sure that old barn office is much better." She glanced out the window—a beautiful layer of snow covered the ground, though the sky was a robin's-egg blue.

"Thomas made her a cradle of sorts and keeps it sitting next to the desk where he can rock her slightly with his foot." *Mammi* peered at Abigail over her half-moon glasses. "I snuck up on him once, and he seems to spend most of his time staring at

Little Jo rather than doing any real work. I think she's claimed his heart."

And suddenly Abigail remembered Thomas holding her hand, speaking to her in a low tone, telling her to get well because Baby Jo needed her, and *Mammi* needed her, and he—Thomas—needed her. She remembered opening her eyes to see him brush away the tears cascading down his cheeks, and then she'd fallen back into the dreamless abyss of the sickness that had claimed her.

"What was wrong with me?"

"Influenza. Doc Amanda has been here twice. She wanted to transfer you to the hospital, but we kept putting her off. I knew you wouldn't want to be away from the baby if at all possible. And if she was going to catch it from you, she already would have. You'd rally enough to nurse Baby Jo..." *Mammi* again paused in her knitting. "You don't remember that?"

"*Nein*. I don't remember much of anything. It feels as if I've lost a week of my life."

"For everything lost there is something gained. Now, let's get you cleaned up."

An hour later, Abigail had washed her hair and changed into fresh clothes. She wanted to go to the kitchen to eat, but felt suddenly, inexplicably exhausted.

"Slow, Abigail. You must go slow." *Mammi* tucked the covers around her. "I'll bring you some toast and tea."

As *Mammi* toddled off, Abigail heard the back door open and close, then the murmur of low voices. Before she could formulate the thought, Thomas appeared in the doorway to her room. He was holding her baby girl.

There was straw in his hair, and a smudge of dirt on his left cheek, but she barely registered those things. Instead, she noticed the warmth in his brown eyes, the way his hair curled at the nape of his neck and the easiness with which he held Baby Jo in the crook of his arm.

"You're awake."

"And you're holding my *boppli* like a natural. The last time I remember asking you to hold her, you'd reminded me that babies could break and nearly run from the room."

"*Ya*. I guess she's not quite as frightening as I made her out to be." He stared down at the bundle in his arms. "I believe I've taught her to sing 'Jingle Bells.'"

Thomas began humming the tune, and Abigail saw two small hands reach up and out of the blanket.

He strode across the room and laid the babe in the crook of her arm. To Abigail's eyes, it seemed that her *doschder* had grown dramatically in the last week. She had more hair than before! Her eyes were wide-open and staring at Abigail, and she waved her arms excitedly, finally plopping her fist into her mouth.

"Still sucking her fist." Thomas pulled the chair closer to the bed and perched on the edge of it.

"I see that."

"She looks like you." His voice was a whisper, a caress really.

"Do you think so?"

"I do." He reached out, ran his hand over the top of Baby Jo's head. "I think you're both beautiful…"

He seemed about to say more, but at that very moment *Mammi* bustled in carrying a tray. Thomas jumped up to help her, then murmured that he needed to go and finish some work in the barn. But he paused at the door, turned back and said, "Five days until Christmas. Lots to do if we're going to be ready."

Baby Jo's first Christmas.

Abigail stared down at her child, then looked back up at Thomas—only he was gone.

"Cookies to bake, gifts to wrap. We'll have a fine celebration." *Mammi* took Baby Jo from her arms and placed her in the cradle. "First, though, we have to get your strength back. Start with the tea and toast. Once we're sure that will stay down, I'll make you some oatmeal."

Abigail ate, nursed Baby Jo and had every intention to continue work on Thomas's winter scarf, but suddenly her eyelids felt as if they had a heavy weight on them.

"Don't fight it, dear."

Mammi took the knitting, slipped it into the project basket, then lowered the shades over the windows. Abigail watched her bustle about, and she realized in that moment how much she was learning from *Mammi*—learning the very things that her *mamm* had never learned from her own mother.

How to show affection.

How to offer comfort with a kind word.

How to simply be with someone in a silent and companionable way.

How to accept help.

Abigail yawned, then curled onto her side, watching the lavender yarn twist and turn as *Mammi* worked her knitting needles.

"Danki, Mammi."

"You're welcome, of course."

"Not just for caring for me while I was sick, but for everything." She yawned again. "For being you. For showing me another way."

Mammi's eyes met hers and she tsked. "There's always another way, a better way, if we're brave enough to embrace it."

Was she?

Was Abigail brave enough to believe that she could be happy? Courageous enough to trust that her future with Baby Jo would be one filled with love and abundance and friends? Could she rely on the goodness of God? And finally, would she be able to embrace the feelings that flooded her heart every time she looked at Thomas?

She wanted to think about all those things, to consider them carefully, but they'd barely passed through her mind when sleep claimed her once again.

Thomas had trouble taking his eyes off Abigail. Only two days ago, the doctor had described her situation as quite grave and insisted that if she didn't improve soon, she'd have to go to the hospital.

It was *Mammi* who had told him not to worry, only believe.

Bishop Luke had reminded them to pray, and then shared a verse of Scripture from the Gospel of Mark. Those words had been rattling around in Thomas's mind for two days.

Lord, I believe; help thou mine unbelief!

That simple line described Thomas perfectly. He did believe the truths found in the Bible, believed every bit of the Christmas story, believed that *Gotte* cared for him and had suffered and died for him. He believed.

But oh, how he pleaded that *Gotte* would help his unbelief.

And He had.

As they prayed silently over the evening meal, Thomas realized that Abigail was living proof of the goodness and provision of *Gotte*.

"Mmm. Smells *gut*." Abigail leaned over the bowl of tomato-basil soup, nearly causing her *kapp* string to fall into it.

Thomas reached forward and brushed it back.

Her eyes met his and she whispered, *"Danki."*

Then Baby Jo let out a grunt and a squeal as an unpleasant odor filled the room. Abigail popped up and reached for her *doschder.*

"I can do that," *Mammi* said.

"You've done enough." Abigail stopped at the little arched entryway between the kitchen and sitting room, then turned to look back. "Unless Thomas would like to…"

"Nein." He was pretty sure he could smell Baby Jo from across the room. "I've done my share of dirty diapers this week. That one's yours."

Abigail's laughter followed her out of the room. Thomas thought if sunshine had a sound, that would be it.

"Are you waiting for Christmas to tell her?"

Thomas didn't even pretend to not know

what she was talking about. He sighed and dipped his spoon into the creamy soup.

"I'm not sure what I'm waiting for," he admitted.

"Christmas is only five days away." *Mammi* bit into her grilled cheese sandwich.

"You think that would be a good time?"

"I wouldn't wait."

"You wouldn't wait five days? Why not? I've waited this long." He crossed his arms and sat back. "Abigail doesn't know what's going to happen with this farm, *Mammi*. And as you know, I live in an apartment above a mercantile. That's not *gut* enough for Abigail or Baby Jo. They deserve a real home."

"A house is made of walls and beams— a home is made of love and dreams."

"Bible?"

She shook her head and turned her attention back to her soup. "*Nein*. Just something my *mamm* used to say."

Abigail returned with a smiling Baby Jo.

The meal passed with talk of the weather and the neighbors and the coming holiday.

Jo began to fuss. Abigail finally pushed away her plate, picked up Baby Jo and placed the child against her shoulder. She rubbed Jo's back in small, gentle circles. Thomas was thinking about that, about how maternal instincts didn't need to be taught—they were there, under the surface, waiting to push through. Was it the same with paternal instincts? Could he be a *gut* father to Little Jo?

"Thomas, did you hear me?"

"*Ya*, of course."

"What did I say?"

"I don't know. My mind was elsewhere, but I did hear you."

Mammi laughed, but when she stood to do the dishes both Abigail and Thomas jumped to their feet.

"Here, *Mammi*. You hold her. She goes to sleep faster with you than with anyone else."

"We'll take care of the dishes," Thomas agreed.

Abigail turned toward him in surprise. "Don't you need to get home?"

"Not really." Thomas realized with a start that the statement was completely true. No one would notice if he wasn't home. Where he stayed wasn't made of love and dreams, as *Mammi* had said. It was simply a few rooms above a mercantile. And that had been fine, for a time. But suddenly it wasn't fine anymore. Suddenly he didn't want to go home. He wanted to stay with Abigail and Baby Jo.

He wanted a family.

Abigail set the stopper in the sink drain, turned on the hot water and squirted soap into it. "I've been thinking about Christmas."

"Have you, now?"

"I have, and I have some ideas." Abigail twirled her hand in the soapy water.

"Oh, boy." He tried to sound put out, but he wasn't fooling anyone. "Just remember you're barely out of bed. You shouldn't try to do too much too soon."

Abigail shrugged, scrubbed a plate and

set it in the rinse water. Thomas plucked it out.

"There are pine trees at the back of the property, right?"

"A nice row of them."

"We could get pine cones and small branches and such. They would make the house smell like Christmas."

"I can do that."

"Oh." Abigail frowned. "I thought we could do it together."

Thomas's pulse accelerated. "Together, *ya*. That's what I meant."

"*Mammi* was talking this afternoon about how when she was a child, they'd string popcorn and cranberries."

"Do you have popcorn?"

"Nope."

"Cranberries?"

"Not even one."

"Sounds like we should go to town."

Now Abigail beamed up at him. "I was hoping you'd say that."

"Sounds like a holly jolly Christmas, but are you sure..." He stared down at the pot he'd been drying for some time, then raised his eyes to Abigail's. "Are you sure you're up to it? I don't want you to overdo things and have a relapse."

"That's sweet of you to worry about me, Thomas."

"Oh, *ya*, well, you know..." Thomas's mind scrambled for something, anything to say. "I guess there's a fine line between taking care of yourself and lounging around sleeping when there's still so much work to be done."

Abigail splashed him with soapy water. "Are you calling me lazy?"

"I'd never say such a thing. Doing so would land me squarely on the naughty list."

"Whose naughty list?"

"Well..." He suddenly wished he hadn't attempted to tease her. How could he focus on what he was saying when she was looking up at him with those brown eyes, when she was smiling at him that way? "Santa's list, perhaps. An Amish Santa. Or maybe it's just Round John wearing a red cap."

Abigail shook her head and returned her attention to the dishes. "Round John could definitely fill in as Santa for the Shipshe Christmas parade."

"You know about that?"

"Last year was the only Christmas I've spent here, and we didn't go—if that's what you're asking. Asher was mostly content to stay on the farm." She focused on the dish she was scrubbing. "But I remember seeing the posters."

Her voice had taken on a pensive tone. Thomas searched for a way to bring the joy back in her voice. Abigail was staring out the window over the sink now. What was she thinking? Was she wishing on a star? If she could have anything, what would it be?

But he knew the answer to that.

She'd already told him, on more than one occasion.

She'd have a perfect first Christmas for her child.

"I like your idea—about making special memories for Baby Jo."

"Ya?" She cocked her head and studied him. "You said it was silly. You pointed out that she won't remember her first Christmas, and I suppose you're right. I don't remember mine."

"She might not remember, but it's not just memories you're making—it's traditions."

"What's the difference?"

"Well, traditions are things we embrace, things we do over and over because they bring us comfort and joy."

"Exactly. That's what I want for Jo. A solid foundation of traditions." She hesitated, then asked, "Does that make me less Amish?"

"Of course not."

"No? Because I also remember someone saying that we aren't *Englisch* and don't celebrate like them."

Thomas rolled his eyes. "That guy sounds like a grinch."

"What do you know about the grinch?"

"Green guy, small heart, bad attitude."

Abigail laughed and pulled the plug on

the dishwater. "I don't know what happened to you while I was sick, but I like it."

"Do you, now?"

"*Ya*, I do."

She stepped closer, looked up at him, and Thomas could no more have stopped himself than he could have willed his heart to quit beating. He bent his head and touched his lips softly to hers.

She didn't step away, and the kiss went on until Baby Jo's cry interrupted the tender moment.

"Sounds like someone is calling you," he said softly.

"I should probably..." But instead of turning away, she stood on tiptoe, put her hands on his face and kissed him again. Thomas experienced a real sense of euphoria. His thoughts turned fuzzy, and his heartbeat kicked up a notch. He forgot about the room they were standing in, the snow outside, his worries over what type of life he could offer Abigail.

He forgot everything except the feel of her in his arms.

Abigail ran her fingers through the hair that curled at his collar, kissed him once more, then turned and bustled out of the room.

Thomas was left trying to figure out exactly when he'd fallen in love with Abigail Yutzy, and what he planned to do about it.

Chapter Thirteen

Abigail woke the next morning feeling like her old self.

She was so full of energy she nearly bolted out of her bed.

Then she remembered Thomas's kiss and the way she had kissed him back. She sank back into her covers and wondered if she had been too bold, but then again...he had started it.

By the time Baby Jo woke, Abigail had dressed and was humming "Joy to the World." As she helped *Mammi* with breakfast, the words to "Away in a Manger" danced through her head. And when she sat on the couch to work on Thomas's scarf, she found herself softly singing "O Come, All Ye Faithful."

"Someone certainly woke up in a Christmas mood," *Mammi* said.

"I did indeed." Why shouldn't she hum? She was recovered from a serious bout of the flu. Baby Jo was flourishing. And Thomas had kissed her after he'd helped her wash dishes. She had kissed him back. Her cheeks warmed at the memory. What had she been thinking?

"Feeling worse?" *Mammi* asked, her brow furrowed in concern.

"*Nein*. At least, not the way you think." She checked the pattern for the scarf, then continued knitting. "How do you know when you're in love?"

"You've been married before, child. I think you know the answer to that question."

"But I wasn't in love with Asher." There was a time when admitting that would have sent a flood of shame through Abigail, but it didn't now. Life had simply turned into something different than she'd imagined, and now it was turning again. Her past was nothing to be ashamed of. "You were in love with your husband. His name was Joshua, right? I can tell you loved him."

"I love him still." The smile on *Mammi*'s face caused her eyes to sparkle.

Or was that tears? But when she looked directly at her, Abigail understood they weren't tears of despair, only memories of joy surfacing once again.

"I knew that I loved Joshua the first time I saw him. We were at a singing in Adam Hochstetler's barn. Joshua was visiting from Ohio. When I looked across and saw him…"

Her voice faded away as the memories overtook her. She stared down at the knitting in her lap, shook her head and resumed her story. "I knew he was the one for me, and I never regretted going over and saying hello, asking him if he'd like to step outside for a cold soda that we kept in coolers. It was bold of me, I knew that, but I couldn't help myself. I wanted to get to know him. I *needed* to get to know him."

"Sounds like the stuff of romance novels."

Mammi shrugged. "The heart knows what it wants. Sometimes we block that out, but other times we listen. *Gotte* blessed me that day, because He caused me to listen to my heart." She tapped her chest. "And my heart told me that Joshua was the one."

"I didn't think Asher was *the* one, but he was *some*one. And my *mamm* and *dat* thought the time had come for me to marry." She finished the row she'd been knitting, turned the scarf over and began to purl. "I don't regret it, though we never shared a love like you and Joshua. Still, Baby Jo is the result of that union."

"A blessing indeed."

"I'll thank the Lord all the days of my life for Asher and for Joanna. As for being in love…" She looked up at *Mammi*, surprised to find the older woman watching her, watching and waiting. "My heart is insisting that I love Thomas, and I believe he may care for me in return."

Mammi clapped her hands. "*Wunderbaar.*"

"I guess." Abigail laughed, then shook her head. "Sometimes, like last night, it seems that he does and that he wants the same things I do. Other times, I'm not so sure. It's as if something causes him to hesitate and then he pulls away."

"Have you asked him why?"

"*Nein.* I assumed he would tell me if he wanted me to know."

"A man can do many things, but I've yet to meet one that can read a woman's mind." *Mammi* stuck her knitting needles into the ball of yarn, stood and stretched her back. She checked on Baby Jo, who was sleeping peacefully, then pointed a crooked finger at Abigail. Playfully scolding her, she said, "Use your words, Abigail Yutzy. If you care for Thomas, tell him so. And if you have questions, ask them. But above all…"

"Listen to my heart?"

"Yes, dear one. Listen to your heart."

The morning passed quickly, and Abigail finished up Thomas's scarf. She tucked it into her sewing basket and pulled out a shawl she had begun for *Mammi*. Only four days until Christmas. What was she thinking starting a project at the last minute?

But her heart told her that *Mammi* would enjoy the pearl-gray-and-soft-pink yarn. She would finish as much as she could, but not stress over it. So what if she gave *Mammi* a half-finished project? They could spend the week between Christmas and New Year's knitting together.

It was a great comfort to her to know that *Mammi* would still be here. When had the older woman become like family? Her presence made the house feel like a home, and her wisdom was something that Abigail sorely needed.

Not that she always agreed with *Mammi*, or Thomas for that matter.

Both thought she should wait one more day to go to town. At lunch, *Mammi* insisted, "Taking a nap might be the better thing to do. Just for a few days. Just to be sure you have your strength back."

Thomas had quickly jumped to *Mammi*'s

side of the discussion. "We will go dashing through the snow—I promise. But tomorrow works better for me anyway. I have... um...work to do in the west field."

"Are you making that up, Thomas Albrecht?"

"*Nein*. I would never do that. And besides...there's always work to do in any field. Ha. Tell me you can argue with that."

She couldn't. She knew that a farmer's work was never done.

Later that afternoon, Clare stopped by to check on her and caught her mopping the floor of the mudroom.

"You must be well. Mudrooms are the last thing I mop. They get dirty again the same hour." They spent a pleasant half hour over a cup of tea while *Mammi* and Baby Jo rested in Jo's room.

As they walked back out onto the front porch, Clare whispered, "You had us all worried—especially Thomas."

Abigail focused on pulling her sweater tighter around her, but she could feel her cheeks flush at the mention of Thomas.

She was still trying to decide what to say when Clare enfolded her in a hug.

"I'm happy for you, Abi."

The only person to call her that had been her *grossdaddi*. Abigail's heart warmed at the memory. She did have good family memories. She could see now that the bulk of them had been buried under a blanket of old hurts and confusion.

"Life is hard. I don't believe we're meant to go it alone, and you and Thomas seem like a natural couple."

"*Danki*, but I don't even know if he feels the same."

"You will know soon enough." Clare's smile widened. "Perhaps he has a Christmas surprise for you."

What could Clare possibly be talking about? It wasn't as if Thomas would drop down on one knee, pull out a diamond ring and ask her to marry him. That was the *Englisch* way. Amish tended to wait until they were walking through a field and the sun was setting. Then they simply popped the question. No ring involved. No fanfare.

Though she supposed the feelings were the same.

The weather was cold, but any additional snow was still holding off. Perhaps they would have a white Christmas. That evening, Thomas missed eating dinner with them because of a fence that had decided to fall down for no apparent reason. He stopped in to tell them good evening and that he was headed home.

Abigail wanted to give him a cup of coffee or hot cocoa, but he'd insisted that he needed to be on his way.

"The fence is done?"

"All mended now." He smiled down at her. "Should we make our trip to town tomorrow?"

"Tomorrow? *Ya.* What time should we be ready?"

"Abigail Yutzy, I have every intention of staying home with Baby Jo." *Mammi* walked into the living room, pulled a sheet of paper from her apron pocket and pressed it into Abigail's hand. "But I did make a list of a few things I'd like you to pick up."

Cinnamon.

Marshmallows.

Peppermint sticks.

"Sweet tooth?" Thomas asked, reading over Abigail's shoulder.

"Ha. Wouldn't you like to know?" *Mammi* walked from the room singing a christmas song.

"She's in the spirit of the season."

"Indeed, she is."

Thomas reached for her hand, causing Abigail's thoughts to scatter. "Can you be ready to leave around nine?"

"Nine will be perfect." Abigail thought he would kiss her again, but *Mammi* picked that moment to walk back into the room and scoop up her glasses from the coffee table. "Can't read without these."

Her smile indicated she knew what she'd interrupted. Thomas laughed, and Abigail pulled in a deep breath. Was this what falling in love felt like? It seemed the day was literally stuffed with anticipation and small joys and hope.

She and *Mammi* had fallen into the habit

of each enjoying a hot cup of herbal tea as Abigail nursed Baby Jo before heading to bed. Lately, she'd taken to reading about the holy birth. *Mammi* opened her worn Bible and read several verses from the prophet Isaiah. Then they spoke of that, of the various names for the Christ Child— Wonderful, Counselor, Mighty God, Everlasting Father, Prince of Peace.

Names mattered.

Those names for the baby Jesus mattered.

And she realized in that moment why she'd insisted on naming her *doschder* Joanna. The word meant *kind*. She'd read that in the baby book that Naomi had given her. Kindness was essential in this life. It was important for a person to both give and receive kindness, and it was something that she was determined to focus on in her parenting of Baby Jo.

She thought she might toss and turn that night, but she fell asleep within minutes of lying down. Her last thought was of the prophet's words and the miracle of her *dos-*

chder. She went to sleep thinking of names and how much kindness she had received in the last few months—enough to believe in the goodness of people again, enough to believe that she was loved and worthy of love. And if you believed that, it seemed to Abigail, anything was possible.

Thomas couldn't remember the last time he'd looked forward to a day in town so much. Normally he was happiest in a barn or a field. When had that changed? Abigail sat beside him in the buggy, going over the lists she'd written. He had to admit that her enthusiasm was contagious.

She glanced up from the pieces of paper she clutched in her gloved hand. "I suppose you'll be with your family on Christmas Day."

"Oh, *ya*. We have one very important tradition that I'm a critical part of. The kids get up early, the parents get tired and Uncle Thomas shows up in time for a big luncheon."

"Your *schweschder* Lily cooks the meal?"

"Most of it, though Grace and Lydia help. After lunch, Grace and Lydia head over to see the other side of the family, and Lily and Josiah sneak off for a nap. That's where my important role comes in. I keep the little ones occupied with their new toys while their parents sleep."

"That does sound like an important tradition." She scrunched up her face. "But I was hoping that we would see you on Christmas."

"Were you, now?"

"I have a present for you," she admitted. "I guess I could give it to you early."

"*Nein*. The best presents you always save for last." He reached for her hand and squeezed it. "I wouldn't miss Baby Jo's first Christmas. I've already told my *schweschdern* that I'll be leaving by three in the afternoon, and I let *Mammi* know that I'll be eating dinner at your place."

"Oh, you have?"

"She invited me… I assumed it was okay with you."

"I suppose." She tapped a finger against

her lips and attempted to look perplexed. "If we can make room. It's going to be crowded with the three of us, but maybe we can squeeze in one more."

He liked this side of Abigail. It did his heart a world of good to see the constant look of worry replaced with holiday cheer.

"Tell me what's on your list there. Where do you want to go?"

They went to Yoder's Department Store first. Thomas followed her around, unsure what he was supposed to do. On the one hand, he could wait in the rocking chairs that lined the middle of the store. That's where most men congregated. On the other hand, he rather liked watching her shop. Though she had access to Asher's bank account now, it was obvious that she was being quite careful with the money. Several times, she'd pick something up, rub her fingers across it, then set it back down with a look of firm resolve.

A few of those things he went back for while she was standing in the checkout line. Then she sat in the rockers while she waited for him to complete his purchases.

"I didn't know you had shopping to do." She bumped her shoulder against his as they made their way back to the buggy.

"Just a few things I realized I needed."

When she tried to peek into his bag, he held it behind his back. "Nosy."

"Guilty."

"You can't see."

"Why not?"

"Because it's a surprise. Christmas is supposed to be full of surprises. Don't you know that?"

She tossed her *kapp* strings over her shoulder and gave him a saucy look. "I know. I have surprises too."

Their next stop was the grocery store, where they consulted both Abigail's list and *Mammi*'s. Soon their cart was filled with a honey-glazed ham, a sack of potatoes, winter squash, three types of cheese, a tin of Hershey's cocoa, cinnamon, marshmallows, peppermint sticks, oranges, nuts, popcorn and cranberries.

When she'd paid for the goods, he insisted on carrying the sacks. "But only if you'll humor me for one more stop."

"I see. You'll help, but only if I do your bidding."

"Exactly."

Instead of turning Duchess toward home, he headed back into town and parked in front of Davis Mercantile.

"Don't tell me you've started quilting."

"*Nein.* We're not headed to Lolly's."

"We're not?" She wriggled her eyebrows. "Second guess—you've taken up knitting and want to purchase some yarn."

"Not even close."

He cupped her elbow with the palm of his hand and led her into the building and toward JoJo's Pretzels. The last time they'd been here was after she'd cleaned out Asher's room, when she'd been physically weighed down with despair. To Thomas it had seemed that she'd been completely overwhelmed at the thought of being a *mamm* and terribly unsure about how things were going to work out.

She still didn't know how they were going to work out.

Neither did Thomas.

That hadn't changed at all.

But they had changed. They'd become something of a family—he and Abigail and Little Jo and even *Mammi*. The only thing left was to make it official.

"Thomas…"

"Huh? What?"

Both Abigail and the girl behind the counter laughed.

"He has Christmas on his mind," Abigail explained.

"We see that a lot here. Now, what can I get you?"

They both ordered a cinnamon pretzel. Then they went to the Kitchen Cupboard, a coffee shop that shared the same retail space. They ordered hot coffees that were served thick with whipped cream on top and little green sprinkles.

"So festive," she said.

"'Tis the season." Thomas raised his mug and clinked it against hers. Christmas music played in the background. Twinkly lights had been strung across the coffee shop, and holiday scenes had been spray-painted on the windows.

Abigail sipped her coffee, studied the room and then smiled at Thomas. It did strange things to his stomach when she focused all of her attention on him. He thought of Mary Lehman reminding him not to wait too long, not to fall into the trap of thinking that there was an endless line of women waiting to marry. He'd never thought that. He'd never considered himself marriage material.

But Mary Lehman was right. No person had infinite chances.

His *schweschdern* had pretty much said the same thing, assuring him that their past was simply that—the past.

Which reminded him of *Mammi* asking what he was waiting for.

"You're seriously studying that pretzel," Abigail said.

"Am I?" He broke off a large chunk and stuffed it in his mouth, which only caused Abigail to laugh like a schoolgirl. She wasn't a schoolgirl, though. She was a beautiful woman who he'd fallen in love with.

"I think I'm in love with you."

She was taking a sip of the coffee, and when she jerked her head up in surprise, she came away with a wide mustache of whipped cream. He smiled and handed her a napkin. "I didn't mean to startle you."

"Startle me?" She opened and closed her mouth twice. Finally, she settled for "I don't know what to say."

"Say you care for me too."

"You know I do." Her voice had dropped to a whisper, but then she sat up straighter, met his gaze and said quite boldly, "I do, Thomas. I do care for you."

"But?"

"But...we're in a coffee shop."

"And?"

"And, you caught me off guard. I'd planned what I would like to say to you, but I thought we'd be taking a moonlit walk through the snow."

Thomas looked out the window, then grinned at her. "Most of the snow is melted."

"Indeed."

"And *Mammi* cautioned me not to wait."

Now Abigail's eyebrows arched. "Did she give you the talk about listening to your heart?"

"*Nein.* She seemed to think I was stalling, but actually I was worried that I couldn't provide for you and Jo. I don't have a real farm, a real home..." He watched Abigail, trying to read her reaction.

"Asher provided me a home, but he never loved me. I understand now that where you live isn't what matters. What matters is how much you care for one another, whether you cherish one another, whether you're kind...not the type of house or the size of the farm."

"*Mammi* reminded me that a home is made of love and dreams." Thomas suddenly wished he hadn't drunk the coffee. The strong brew felt acidic in his stomach as the old doubts rose up to meet the dark brew. "Abigail, there's something I need to tell you before...well, before this goes any further. It might change how you feel."

"Nothing can change how I feel, Thomas."

He nodded in agreement, but his words voiced his fear that the opposite might be true. "I know you believe that, but hear me out. There's a reason I haven't married. There's a reason that I thought I'd never make a good husband or a good father."

"Baby Jo loves you."

"And I love her. I really do. I had no idea that I could feel so...protective toward a *boppli.*" He crossed his arms on the table, determined to get through this. "My family, growing up, it wasn't what a family should be."

"You've hinted at that before."

"My *dat* was an alcoholic."

The voices around them had faded into the background, until it seemed to Thomas that it was just him and Abigail sitting there together. Suddenly it wasn't so difficult to pour out the doubts that he had so carefully stored in his heart.

"It was terrible—truly. We never knew if there'd be enough money for food or proper clothes. My parents insisted on hiding it from our church, so the bishop and elders didn't know how dire the situation was." He shook his head at the memories. In some ways those days seemed as if they'd occurred last week, and in other ways they seemed as if they'd happened to someone else.

"That must have been terribly hard for you. My parents were emotionally distant, but they always provided for us."

"Occasionally someone would understand the seriousness of our situation and try to help. My *dat* would rudely assure them that we were fine, but we weren't fine. My *mamm* wasn't. My *schweschdern* weren't. I wasn't." The admission brought him freedom. It was as if he'd been carrying around a giant weight and had just realized he could set it down. "I became the man of the house at a very young age."

"Both of your parents have passed?"

"*Ya*. My *dat* when I was only twelve. My *mamm* a few years ago."

"I'm sorry."

"Here's the thing. I've done some reading on the subject, and doctors agree that sometimes alcoholism can be genetic."

"I've never seen you drink."

"I don't, but what if I have the gene? What if it's something that just…switches on when you turn forty, like high cholesterol or male-pattern baldness?"

"You're going to be bald?" Her voice was teasing, but her eyes couldn't have been more serious. She reached across the table and covered his hands with her own. "You are a *gut* man, Thomas. And I know, in my heart of hearts, that you'd be a *gut* husband and an excellent father."

Oh, how he wanted to believe that.

Somehow, looking at Abigail with her hands covering his, he could. He didn't know what had caused his own *dat* to choose the wrong path. Perhaps it had been a sickness that he couldn't overcome. Maybe he'd been weak willed. Possibly he hadn't known of the danger that waited for him behind that first bottle.

But Thomas knew. He'd be vigilant. He wouldn't let anything come between him and his family.

"If I ever..."

"You won't."

"But if I did..."

"Then we would face it together. I wouldn't hide it from others, Thomas. I don't know why your *mamm* did, but I know I wouldn't. We have friends and family and a church that cares about us, and they're on the inside of our lives where they belong. We won't push them out, no matter what problems we face."

And those words convinced him more than anything else.

Abigail had been through the worst that a young woman could experience—a loveless marriage, the untimely death of her husband, being a single mother, being penniless. Instead of breaking her spirit, those things had made her stronger. They'd helped her become the woman who was sitting across from him.

She cleared her throat. "There is one more thing we haven't discussed, though."

"I can't imagine anything else that would possibly matter." He offered her a sheepish grin. "I was worried you didn't feel the same."

Her smile was a reflection of his, but it quickly dimmed. "We still don't know how the probate of Asher's estate is going to turn out. I thought I'd hear this week..."

"It doesn't matter."

"It does matter. After learning how indebted Asher was... Well, I don't understand what I'm supposed to do with that. I haven't the vaguest idea of where Baby Jo and I will live if we lose the farm."

"It's something we can figure out together." He waited until she stopped staring into her coffee. "If I can trust you with my past, my history, you can trust me with your future."

"*Ya.* You're right, Thomas. I can."

They walked toward his buggy arm in

arm, surrounded by shops that were decked out for Christmas. It was the most joyous time of the year, and Thomas felt that joy inside him.

They stopped beside the buggy. Abigail reached up and kissed him softly, gently on the lips. His doubts and fears fled, and he was filled with a sense of calm.

He understood that there were many important decisions ahead of them. They'd make them together. By this time next year he'd have a family of his own, and they'd celebrate the season together.

Chapter Fourteen

Abigail stood staring at the coffeepot brewing on the stove, her heart and mind full of far too many emotions and thoughts.

"The coffee goes in the cup." *Mammi* reached around her for one of the mugs.

"I'm feeling a bit overwhelmed," Abigail admitted.

"All you have to do, at any given moment, is the next thing." *Mammi* held up the pot. "Coffee?"

"*Ya.* That's definitely the next thing."

She'd told *Mammi* about her conversation with Thomas. *Mammi* had clapped her hands and sent a "praise the Lord" up to the heavens. When Abigail cautioned her that there were still a lot of details to work out, *Mammi* had nodded in understanding, then smiled and offered, "Faith makes things possible, not easy."

That pretty much said it all.

Abigail added a touch of cream to her coffee and sank into a chair at the table.

Mammi peered over her own cup of coffee. "How did Baby Jo sleep?"

"*Gut.* She woke me an hour ago to feed her, and now she's fast asleep." The sky was just beginning to lighten, though clouds pressed heavily across the horizon—snow clouds if she wasn't mistaken. "It's Christmas Eve."

"Yes, it is."

"I feel excited and happy and a little... pensive."

Mammi sipped her coffee and waited.

"I was supposed to hear from the lawyer this week."

"Yup. Are you worried?"

"Not really. It just feels as if the New Year is going to be full of changes, and

I have no idea which way those changes might take me."

"True." *Mammi* patted her hand. "But you do know who will be with you on your new path."

Leave it to *Mammi* to correct her train of thought. Regardless of what news the attorney brought, she wouldn't be alone. She'd have Jo and *Mammi*…and Thomas. That realization did more than ease her worries. It put a song in her heart.

She dressed Jo in a warm onesie and added a stocking *kapp* she'd knit—it was red with white hearts and to Abigail's way of thinking looked very festive. A year ago, she hadn't known how to knit. Now she was knitting garments for her *doschder*. It was amazing the changes that a short time could bring.

Changes in her abilities.

Changes in her heart.

Thomas stopped by midmorning. By that point, they were stringing popcorn with cranberries. Baby Jo lay in her playpen, waving her arms and looking as if she approved of the new decorations.

Mammi made brownies topped with broken peppermint.

Thomas and Abigail fetched pine boughs and stretched them across the mantel, windowsills and bookshelves. They filled the air with the scent of winter and Christmas and celebration.

It was as she was clearing up the lunch dishes that a car pulled up in front of the house. Gabriela Martinez stepped out.

Thomas tried to leave them alone to discuss the probate, but Abigail wanted him with her. She wanted her entire family with her. So it was that Thomas sat across from her, holding Baby Jo. *Mammi* sat to her right, her old weathered Bible on the table in front of her. Gabriela sat on her left, a large envelope filled with papers in front of her.

"It isn't what we hoped," she said right away. "But it's not as bad as it could have been."

Abigail had no idea how to answer that, so she didn't.

"Given the degree of indebtedness and the fact that you have no prospect of a regular income, the judge has ordered that the farm be placed up for auction after the first of the year."

Abigail blinked, but still couldn't speak. It could have been worse.

"The good news is that the balance of the funds in the account will remain yours, as will the items in the house, the livestock and the buggy." She looked up from the papers. "I must say that I agree with the judge's ruling. A farm this size, it's probably more than a single mom would want to deal with. And the fact that it's going to auction means that you don't have to worry about finding a buyer or settling the debts."

She pulled out more papers. "As we discussed earlier, I filled out a bankruptcy petition and presented it to the judge. He approved it, Abigail. You can effectively walk away from Asher's bad business decisions. You can have a new beginning, though the bankruptcy will remain on your credit history. You might have trouble procuring a loan, at least for the next ten years, since this was a Chapter 7 bankruptcy."

Abigail pulled in a deep breath. Glancing out the window, she saw that it had begun to snow. Christmas Eve, fresh snow and court papers to sign. Those three things didn't seem to go together, yet here she was. And then she remembered *Mammi*'s words from earlier that morning:

All you have to do, at any given moment, is the next thing.

With a smile and a prayer, she picked up a pen, and she began to sign the forms.

Thomas stood on the front porch with her as they watched Gabriela drive away.

He reached for her hand. "Are you upset?"

"Surprisingly, I'm not."

"Worried?"

She shook her head, then gazed up into his eyes. *"Nein."*

"I love you, Abigail Yutzy."

"And I love you, Thomas Albrecht."

"We'll start over. Start fresh. I have some money saved, enough for a good down payment on a place."

"And unlike me, you have a good credit history."

"I do, though you know…" he traced her jawline with his thumb, then bent to kiss her lips "…I've heard Amish don't like to go into debt."

"You are correct. We don't." She stood on tiptoe and kissed him back. "Too bad you're not going to get paid for all that work you did on the Yutzy place."

"I'm getting paid. There's an entire plate of brownies in there, and I plan on eating my fair share."

"Uh-huh."

"Would you look at that?" He turned her around, so that she was facing toward the fields and his arms were snug around her. "It's really starting to come down."

"A fresh snow…for Christmas."

Baby Jo let out a shout from inside the house. Abigail pivoted in Thomas's arms again and smiled up at him. "Sounds like our baby girl is ready to begin celebrating."

"Indeed, it does."

They walked into the house as the snow continued to fall and the evening darkened. *Mammi* was sitting in her rocker and the room was cozy from the fire in the big black stove. The room smelled of baking and wood fires, pine boughs and Christmas. It smelled like home, though it wasn't Thomas's home and never would be.

But these people were his home, and the fact that they wouldn't be in this place for the coming year didn't really matter at all. They'd be together, and that was far more important than the location.

It was difficult for Thomas to leave that evening, but he did because Baby Jo was snoozing softly, *Mammi* had already gone to bed and Abigail looked as if she could barely keep her eyes open.

He kissed her at the door. "I'm getting used to this."

"My falling asleep on you?"

"Kissing."

"Oh, *ya*." She stifled a yawn, then snugged herself into his arms. "Me too."

"Merry Christmas," he whispered.

"It's not Christmas yet."

"I know, but I wanted to be the first to say it to you."

He kissed her again, then slipped out into the night. When he reached his home, he stopped over at the Lehmans'. They'd made it a policy long ago not to exchange gifts, but every Christmas Eve, he enjoyed a cup of coffee and slice of pie with them. All the children were there, and Chloe was atwitter with details of her newest boyfriend. It seemed like just the other day Thomas had been avoiding the family because of her crush on him. Time had moved them all along.

When he was alone in the kitchen with John and Mary, he caught them up on the happenings in his life.

"I'm happy for you, Thomas. Abigail sounds like a lovely person, and it's plain as the peaches in that pie how much you care about her."

"I've never heard love compared to pie before."

"What my *fraa* is saying is that we love you like a son, and if there's ever anything we can do for you and your new family—you let us know."

"Actually..."

He stayed another hour as they hammered out the details. Then he borrowed some plain brown wrapping paper and a spool of bright green ribbon and hurried home to wrap his gifts.

The next morning with his *schweschdern* and their children was as special as it had always been. He didn't have to tell everyone that he had big news. As soon as he walked through the door, Lily said, "Oh, *bruder.* I can tell you have something to say. You're practically bursting to share it. I know! A Christmas wedding. Just like I had hoped."

"Someone's getting married today?" He'd picked up his infant nephew, who he was no longer afraid to hold. "Is it you, Fremont? Are you getting married?"

His nieces and nephews thought that was hilarious, but his *schweschdern* wouldn't be satisfied until he'd told them every detail of his conversation with Abigail in the coffee shop. Everyone congratulated him, even his nieces and nephews. They celebrated Christmas with the reading of the Christmas story, gifts and a *wunderbaar* meal.

The day passed in a blur—Thomas's thoughts hopping between the loved ones in front of him and the loved ones that he was eager to go and see. Grace and Lydia left with their families to visit their in-laws, and Lily and Josiah snuck off for their traditional Christmas afternoon nap.

Thomas was only on his third game of checkers, kids spread around him and the baby in his lap, when Lily came back into the room, claiming the baby. "Go. Go see her."

"But…"

"Just go before I change my mind." She yawned, then smiled. "I think I need another cup of coffee."

Duchess seemed quite content to clip-clop down the road on a bright Christmas afternoon. They passed Amish and *Englisch* families alike who were outside, enjoying snowball fights and making angels in the snow. His heart lightened as he turned down Abigail's lane. If she was surprised to see him so early, she didn't say anything about it.

"Say, that's a lot of presents you have there."

It wasn't. It was five presents, and three of them were for Baby Jo.

Abigail and *Mammi* both cooed over the bouncy seat, play quilt that had mirrors and rattlers and stuffed animals sewn on it, and basket full of tub toys.

"I think someone was spying on me at Yoder's the other day. I seem to remember looking at each of these things."

"Maybe. I'm not saying I would spy on you, but maybe that's the way it happened."

Mammi gave him a knitted toboggan hat which just happened to match the scarf that Abigail gave him.

"I'm ready for any winter storm now."

He gave *Mammi* a beautifully braided cord to wear and attach her glasses to. "Woven from alpaca yarn. I thought you could appreciate that since it's—you know—handmade and natural."

"Very kind of you," *Mammi* said, reaching up to kiss his cheek. "Now you should give Abigail her gift before she snatches it away."

"I wasn't going to snatch."

"You do look a bit impatient."

"I suppose I might snatch, if you keep teasing me."

He'd spent an inordinate amount of time on the bow for her package, but it still looked like what it was—homemade. Abigail didn't notice. She pulled on one end, unwound the green ribbon, then slipped it into her pocket. "That'll make a nice hair ribbon," she said.

He could just see it, braided through her hair.

She slid a finger under the pieces of tape and carefully unwrapped the present. She ran her finger over the words on the cover—Mom's First Journal—then looked up at him, tears sparkling in her eyes. "It's lovely. Thank you."

"Read the inside." He scooted beside her on the couch, and when she opened the cover, together they read the words he'd inscribed there.

When you reach the last page, I'll buy you another. And another. And another...

Instead of remarking on the gift, Abigail pulled him closer and kissed his cheek.

"She likes it," *Mammi* remarked.

It was later that evening, as he was sitting on the couch with Abigail, a fire warming the room, and candles lit on the mantel, that he told her of his plan. *Mammi* had retired, looking happy but tired. Baby Jo lay asleep on Abigail's lap. He claimed her tiny hand in his.

"I spoke with Mary and John last night. Mary and John Lehman."

"The couple who owns the mercantile."

"And my apartment—yes. You'll like the Lehmans. They're *gut* people. A kind family and strong in their faith."

"You talked to them about...us?"

"I did. I told them that we love each other and want to marry. You do want to marry me. Don't you, Abigail?"

"I do."

"Whew." He pretended to wipe sweat off his brow, then once again became serious. "I asked them if I could purchase five acres of their land. It would be enough to build a house, with rooms for us and *Mammi* and any future children..."

"Five acres would be plenty. We'd have room for our horses and a garden."

"And a dog, if Baby Jo wants one." He slipped an arm around Abigail, pulling her close. Baby Jo was still in her arms, and so he felt that their family made a tight little circle. "I have enough money saved for five acres. I could pay cash."

"We don't need any more than that. Not if you intend to keep being an Amish property manager."

"Someone once told me I'm pretty *gut* at it."

"I could provide a solid reference." She snuggled closer.

"Would it be enough? A small place? It's certainly not traditional."

"Our family isn't traditional," Abigail pointed out. "But it's all I want—a place to raise Baby Jo, an extra room for *Mammi*, space for our family to grow."

In that moment, Thomas let go the last of his doubts. He had a family now—people who cared about him, people he loved and wanted around him always. It was the best Christmas gift he could have wished for and one that promised to keep on giving him the most important things in his life.

Love.

Joy.

Happiness.

Kindness.

There really wasn't a single other thing that they needed.

* * * * *

*If you loved this story,
pick up the other books in the
Indiana Amish Brides series,*

A Widow's Hope
Amish Christmas Memories
A Perfect Amish Match
The Amish Christmas Matchmaker
An Unlikely Amish Match
The Amish Christmas Secret
The Baby Next Door

*from bestselling author
Vannetta Chapman*

*Available now from Love Inspired!
Find more great reads at
www.LoveInspired.com*

Dear Reader,

Have you ever had your circumstances take a terrible turn? One that seems impossible to recover from? One that shakes your faith and leaves you feeling alone and frightened?

Abigail Yutzy experiences that in her life when her husband of less than a year dies. Though Asher wasn't the husband she'd dreamed he might be, they were a family. Now she's alone and expecting her first child.

Thomas Albrecht came from a home damaged by alcoholism. His fear is that he will become what his father was. He doesn't trust himself to fall in love, to hope of a future or dream of a family.

But God has a plan for Abigail and Thomas, just as He has a plan for you and for me. And He can be trusted to be with us while we hurt, to be near, and to guide us into what comes next.

I hope you enjoyed reading *An Amish*

Baby for Christmas. I welcome comments and letters at vannettachapman@gmail.com.

May we continue "giving thanks always for all things unto God and the Father in the name of our Lord Jesus Christ" (Ephesians 5:20).

Blessings,
Vannetta